"Wait, don't go in yet," Danny said, springing to his feet. He walked over to the doorway where Katherine was standing. "I want—"

"What do you want, Danny?"

"I don't know. Yes, I do." He caught a strand of her silver hair and brushed it back from her forehead. "I want to touch your hair. I want to feel you against me. I want to . . ." He groaned. "Ah, Katherine, I don't know if I can keep away from you."

"I know," she murmured, and leaned against the wall. She swallowed hard and tried not to tremble. Yes, she wanted her son. But more and more, she couldn't escape the knowledge that she also wanted Danny. Ten years alone had taught her enough to understand how much she wanted him.

She felt his warm breath on her hair. A muted word slipped out as his hands slid around her waist and pulled her against him.

"Ah, Katherine."

This time when he kissed her it wasn't rough, it wasn't quick, and it definitely wasn't a simple good night. . . .

WHAT ARE *LOVESWEPT* ROMANCES?

They are stories of true romance and touching emotion. We believe those two very important ingredients are constants in our highly sensual and very believable stories in the *LOVESWEPT* line. Our goal is to give you, the reader, stories of consistently high quality that may sometimes make you laugh, sometimes make you cry, but are always fresh and creative and contain many delightful surprises within their pages.

Most romance fans read an enormous number of books. Those they truly love, they keep. Others may be traded with friends and soon forgotten. We hope that each *LOVESWEPT* romance will be a treasure—a "keeper." We will always try to publish

LOVE STORIES YOU'LL NEVER FORGET
BY AUTHORS YOU'LL ALWAYS REMEMBER

The Editors

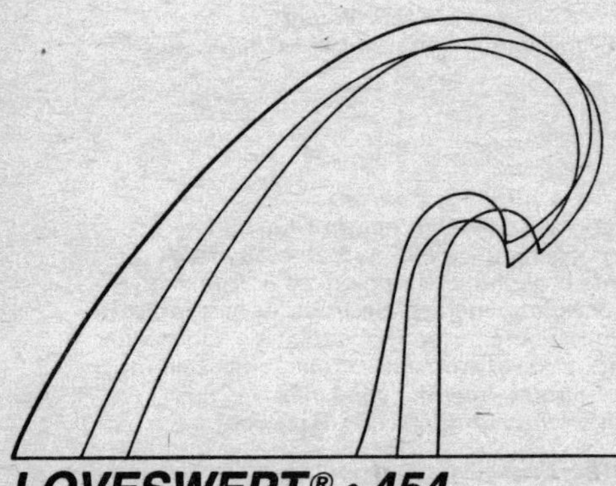

LOVESWEPT® • 454

Sandra Chastain

Danny's Girl

BANTAM BOOKS
NEW YORK • TORONTO • LONDON • SYDNEY • AUCKLAND

DANNY'S GIRL

A Bantam Book / February 1991

LOVESWEPT® and the wave device are registered trademarks of Bantam Books, a division of Bantam Doubleday Dell Publishing Group, Inc. Registered in U.S. Patent and Trademark Office and elsewhere.

If you would be interested in receiving protective vinyl covers for your Loveswept books, please write to this address for information:

Loveswept
Bantam Books
P. O. Box 985
Hicksville, NY 11802

ISBN 0-553-44099-3

Published simultaneously in the United States and Canada

Bantam Books are published by Bantam Books, a division of Bantam Doubleday Dell Publishing Group, Inc. Its trademark, consisting of the words "Bantam Books" and the portrayal of a rooster, is Registered in U.S. Patent and Trademark Office and in other countries. Marca Registrada. Bantam Books, 666 Fifth Avenue, New York, New York 10103.

PRINTED IN THE UNITED STATES OF AMERICA

OPM 0 9 8 7 6 5 4 3 2 1

One

Meet me at our place at midnight.

There was no postage mark on the envelope. It hadn't been mailed.

There was no signature on the note. Katherine Sinclair didn't need one.

Slowly Katherine crumpled the letter in her hand, the crackling of the paper jarring the stillness of the morning.

Beyond the porch she watched Mike as he stood on the diving board fearlessly forming his nine-year-old body into an arched curve before giving up and plunging into the pool crossed-legged and bottom first. Surfacing, he glanced up, as he often did, just to see if she was watching, and gave her a big grin.

When he pulled himself from the water and headed back to the board again, she felt a swell of love wash over her. Mike—her son, the son who had been lost to her for most of his life—was hers again, even if he didn't know yet that she was his mother.

Now Danny was back. Fear shot through her, along with the quivery feeling that she was being watched by secret eyes from the shadows beyond. She forced herself to sit in the sunshine and continued to rock evenly, rhythmically, steadfastly refusing to think about the change in direction of her life.

First had come the message from the attorney that Mike's adoptive parents had been killed. Now six months later, after she'd at last found the son she'd given up when she was seventeen, she'd received this cryptic message from his father.

"What's wrong, Katherine?"

Katherine looked over at her Aunt Victoria, who was sorting the remainder of the morning mail.

A long silent moment passed before Katherine could answer. She wasn't prepared. She hadn't expected to see or hear from Danny again.

"Danny Dark's come home. He wants to see me—tonight."

Katherine stood and walked to the end of the sun room. She stared out into the garden, absently threading her fingertips through her hair, reducing the neat, swept-back style into a tousled mass of silver that flared about her face. She looked as if she were six years old again, flying through the afternoon on her bicycle.

To Aunt Vic's credit she didn't push for details, nor did she elaborate on her thoughts. Aunt Vic. If it hadn't been for her ten years before, Katherine might not have had the strength to survive the decision to let her baby be adopted.

Though it had seared her heart with an open

wound that had never fully healed, Katherine had been convinced, even then, that providing a stable home with two loving parents was the right thing for her son. Making the choice to give him up had nearly destroyed her spirit, but she'd done it. She'd made a life for herself, too, a secure, controlled, lonely life—until she'd been given another chance.

There'd never been a question in her mind about bringing Mike home. She just hadn't been able to find a way to explain to him that the parents he'd always loved weren't his real family at all. It was still too soon.

"Well, I'm not going to meet him, Aunt Vic. I can't. Who does Danny Dark think he is? Ten years ago I waited for him. He never came then, or in all the years since. Now he just waltzes into town and expects me to come running to him?"

"Presumptuous of him," Victoria agreed, "but then he always was sure of himself with you, wasn't he?"

"Well, not this time." Katherine gave a small sigh. "I have no intention of meeting Danny Dark by the river at midnight. I have no intention of meeting him at all."

"Katherine, I don't mean to interfere, but don't you think you ought to tell him what's happened? I mean, about Mike?"

"Absolutely not, Aunt Vic. For so many years I wanted to tell him, but he forfeited the right to know. He doesn't deserve the truth. Oh, Aunt Vic, why did he have to come back now. I haven't even figured out how to tell Mike that I'm his real mother. Meeting Danny will only complicate the situation."

"You're right, of course. Sneaking out to meet Danny in the middle of the night would be as foolish now as it was then. Why not meet him in your office? That is, if you care what he has to say."

If she cared? The irony of Aunt Vic's words was lost in the unsettling thought of seeing Danny again. A shiver of fear and unrestrained excitement ran over her, followed by desperate anguish. If the wild pumping of her heart was any measure, meeting Danny would be a mistake, wherever it happened.

Why had he come back? Why hadn't he sent that note ten years ago? She'd waited for his letter, watched for it until her eyes ached, until her mind refused to find excuses for its absence any longer. When she'd needed him most, he hadn't been there for her. Now, with no warning, he'd suddenly appeared.

Katherine smoothed out the note, refolded the paper, and slid it back into its jacket, as if by closing it away her senses would be controlled. Unless Danny had business in Dark River, they didn't have anything to say to each other. And business was discussed in an office, not in a secret place at midnight. It was years too late to believe there could be anything else between them. She wasn't seventeen anymore.

"Well," Aunt Vic went on indifferently, "if he's in town, I don't see how you're going to avoid him. Maybe it would be better for you to call the shots." She tucked the remainder of the mail into her apron pocket. "I say the mayor of Dark River, Georgia can make her own choices. Though, if she is going to meet with the Garden Club for lunch, she'd better get a move on."

"Ugh! More chicken salad and Jell-O." Katherine drew her attention back to the present.

" 'Fraid so, darling. When they voted down my suggestion to change to tacos and tequila, I resigned. Personally, I thought that a little change would be good for the soul, to say nothing for the rest of the body."

"Aunt Vic!" Katherine ignored her aunt's remark. "Steak and french fries with the Jaycees tomorrow is about as lively as it's going to get in this town, I'm afraid. At least steak and potatoes are safer than cupcakes and soda pop." Katherine started to drop the note in the wastebasket, then drew her hand back.

"What are you really scared of, Katherine?"

Of Danny Dark, she almost said, then stopped in midstep and bit back the reply. "Of myself, Aunt Vic. I'd better get going." Katherine crushed the paper even smaller in her hand and went to the door, calling out, "I'm leaving for the office, Mike. See you later."

"Sure, Katherine," he said with a broad grin and a wave.

Katherine took one last look at her son and was filled with pride. Mike was a tough kid, just like his father. He was handling the death of his adoptive parents well. He'd been surprised when Katherine had explained that she was a close friend of his mother and that it was his parents' wish that he come live in Dark River. After a few weeks Mike had seemed to adjust, and now Katherine couldn't imagine life without him.

In the beginning Katherine had been afraid that the shock of learning she was his birth mother might be too much for the grieving boy. Then, later, the task of telling him had become more difficult. Every day he claimed a bigger chunk of her heart, and every day she felt her fear of losing him grow. At night she sat by his bed, just listening to the sound of him breathing—this son she'd almost lost.

Had Danny returned to claim Mike? She'd fight for him with her last ounce of strength!

Katherine Sinclair wasn't a frightened young girl now. She was the mayor of Dark River, and she'd outgrown cupcakes and soda pop a long time ago—and the boy who'd brought them to private picnics on the bank of the river.

And she was too grown-up to attend the monthly Garden Club luncheon wearing sandals and a sundress, even if it was June-hot and humid. As the mayor she had an image to maintain. And this day, especially, she felt a need to present an official face to her small town.

Thirty minutes later she was headed toward the Dark River Inn. As she drove she cast her eyes toward the old houses that lined the shady road. Though Dark River adjoined the city of Savannah, it was and always had been unique. Graceful old live oaks sent bent arms skyward, draped with wisps of Spanish moss. Rich black dirt nurtured flowers in exotic gardens alongside streets peopled with families that had lived there for generations. Bordered on the east by the Atlantic and on the west by Dark River, her town was a tiny pocket of the past, clinging to tradition, changing little in more than two hundred years.

The man standing in her office doorway the next afternoon had changed a great deal. He wasn't the tough-looking, wise-cracking kid he'd been at seventeen. This Danny Dark could have stepped off the pages of *Gentleman's Quarterly*. Wearing a cream-colored silk jacket, expensive casual cotton slacks, and an open-neck shirt, he was no longer the thin, intense boy Katherine had once known. Over ten years his lanky frame had filled out, giving him a certain self-confidence that spilled over into the way he stood, the way he spoke.

"Hello, Katherine. It's been a long time."

His voice had deepened. A simple hello was all he'd offered, yet he just as easily could have been inviting her into his arms. But it wasn't the voice or the words that reached out and touched her, it was his eyes—dark, hypnotic, intense. She felt the familiar raw power of his presence as if they were still seventeen, standing by the river.

"Danny," she said as evenly as her soft voice would allow, "it's been ten years, almost exactly."

"Call me Dan, Katherine. Danny makes me feel

seventeen again, and it's hard enough facing the good citizens of Dark River, Georgia at twenty-seven."

"You always did make molehills into mountains—Dan. There probably aren't many people around Dark River who still remember you. The young ones have gone, and many of the older ones have died. Besides, you used to say that you didn't care what people thought about you."

"Yes, I did," he said softly, "too much."

"I know. Come in, Danny."

Dan Dark suddenly became Danny again as memories rushed past his defenses, firing the long-buried ache deep within him. He nodded and followed her directions, coming to a stop behind one of the high-backed chairs beside her desk.

Cool, calm, polished, Katherine's image was that of reserve. The fragile uncertainty he remembered was gone. This woman was a study in control and beauty. For a long moment he only stared. He felt the wall between them, invisible but solid. How could he have thought that meeting her again would be easy?

Katherine Sinclair was a beautiful woman. Skin the color of peaches hadn't changed. But the flawless face had matured into a countenance that defied any cursory glance. Under his gaze, Katherine blinked, her cheeks blushing a telltale pink, a sign of emotion she never could control. Dan gave an inward sigh of relief.

He could tell that Katherine wasn't having any easier a time of this than he, in spite of her attempt to appear otherwise. Her eyes, blue as a summer sky, churned now with veiled confusion that threatened her calm restraint. But it was her hair, her glorious hair, gold in the sunshine and silver in the moonlight, that stunned him into a state of foolish fantasy. He'd thought the memory of that hair sprawled free across his chest had lost its hold on him.

He was wrong.

Only the sound of their breathing broke the silence. They stared at each other for a quiet moment, a moment lasting a fraction too long.

Dan felt his lips narrowing into a familiar line he knew Katherine would remember well. His frown always signaled his frustration. Even knowing he was revealing his emotional state, he couldn't force his lips to relax. Dammit, he could calm a boardroom filled with the opposition, but she always could drive him wild.

Danny searched Katherine's face for some clue to her feelings. He didn't know what was wrong. When the strange telephone call had come from Victoria Willingham, Katherine's aunt, he'd been surprised. When she'd told him Katherine was in trouble and needed him, he hadn't stopped to think. He'd made arrangements for his assistant to take over the company temporarily, and he'd come. He'd wanted an excuse to return to Dark River for ten years.

What was wrong? Katherine was tense. She was too cool. He'd expected her to be angry with him as she had every right to be. He'd expected her to demand explanations. He was still angry with himself over how he'd treated her. But instead he sensed fear, fear she was making a valiant attempt to hide. He could identify with that only too well.

Danny Dark was a master at hiding his emotions. He'd spent the better part of his life doing so, first as a smart kid, later as a rebellious teenager. By pretending that it didn't matter what people thought about him, he'd lied to himself about his feelings. He wouldn't do that now. He might have turned his back on Katherine once. He wouldn't make that mistake again.

Dan drew his brows together. This was no way to gain Katherine's confidence. All during breakfast at the Dark River Inn his expectations had swung from wanton fantasy to cool speculation over how to approach her. Multimillion-dollar deals were child's play for him, but facing Katherine again was hard.

"You're not married?" he asked finally.

"No."

Damn, why had he asked that question? He knew Katherine wasn't married. Aunt Vic had told him. He also knew she'd had a career as a journalist before coming back to Dark River, how she'd worked with the radio station and the civic groups before being elected mayor of the small city. At twenty-seven she was successful and single. So was he.

With grim determination Dan forced himself to relax and sit down in the chair he'd been leaning against. He badly needed to appear warm and friendly—neither trait came easily to him. This meeting wasn't going in the direction he'd envisioned. Just seeing Katherine had blasted his logical plan into smithereens.

Aunt Vic had been so mysterious that he'd had no clue as to how to approach Katherine. He'd tried the sentimental approach with his note. But that hadn't worked. The note had only made her skittish and wary. He didn't know what was wrong, but he'd been warned that Katherine had to be the one to tell him, that he had to make her want to confide in him. To complicate matters, one glance had told him his feelings hadn't changed. In his heart Katherine Sinclair was still Danny's girl.

Ten years ago he'd been forced to leave Dark River and Katherine. Now he had to get past his guilt so he could get to know her again. The only problem was that he didn't have a lot of time. He had a business trip to Saudi Arabia in less than a month.

A pulse flexed in his temple. Danny looked at the uncertainty in Katherine's eyes and searched for a way to reclaim some of the ease they'd once had together. She'd been his staunch defender through most of their lives. There had to be answers and forgiveness for both of them. They owed each other that much. They owed each other the truth.

"Why are you here, Danny? We aren't teenagers anymore, either one of us."

"No, this might be easier if we were. I came back to Dark River for two reasons, Katherine. Seeing you again is one of them."

Katherine cleared her throat and pretended she hadn't heard what he'd said.

The tightening of her facial muscles told Danny she wasn't going to make it easy. He strummed his fingers on the chair arm. "About the note, I'm sorry. I shouldn't have written it. I was afraid you wouldn't see me. I just wanted to talk to the Katherine I once knew. That was a mistake. I was wrong to try to play on memories."

"Yes, you were. You said there were two reasons?"

During the time he'd waited outside her office, Danny had decided he'd take it slow, one step at a time, as he would with any unknown adversary. This woman was Katherine, but she wasn't the girl he'd known. She was guarded and distant. For now he didn't have to let her know he was there to see her through whatever trouble she was facing.

Danny had already discovered the one ingredient he hadn't taken into account, at least not consciously. There was still something between them. He wasn't certain yet what it was, but he was willing to gamble that their shared past was enough to build pathways to the present.

But any hope of gentle explanations suddenly vanished in the wake of a rush of footsteps in the outer office and the clatter of noise in the doorway.

Mike burst into the office. "Katherine, guess what? Down at the barbershop there's a real Revolutionary War battle set up with Whigs and Tories and ships in a river. The grown-ups play with it—not kids. Aunt Vic talked Fred, the barber, into letting me look at it."

"Katherine? Aunt Vic?" Danny took a close look at the boy, and his heart plummeted. The boy had golden hair and blue eyes, just like Katherine. Danny gasped. He couldn't seem to pull air into his lungs. It couldn't be. Katherine had a child? A son? The thought kept slamming around in his mind like an out-of-control bumper car at an amusement park.

Behind the desk Katherine felt a kaleidoscope of feeling rush through her. Danny, the person she had once wanted more than anything else in her life, was back, and now he'd know her secret. One look at his face when he'd seen Mike told her that he was as stunned as she. From the moment the lawyer who'd handled Mike's private adoption had called her, she'd feared what might happen if Danny ever returned. By claiming Mike, she ran the risk that one day Danny would learn the truth. She just hadn't expected him to crash into it unexpectedly—before she was ready.

Katherine held back the impulse to rush Mike outside and spoke in what she hoped would be a normal voice. "Mike, you know you're supposed to check with my secretary, Nancy, before you come into my office."

"Oh, gosh, I forgot. But Nancy's gone, and Aunt Vic had some more shopping to do. I was supposed to wait in the park. But, hey, I saw you through the window and . . . I'm sorry, Katherine. There are some really neat places in Dark River. There's a drugstore that makes soft drinks with syrup and carbonated water, by hand, like in the olden days. I just got overexcited, I guess."

Even though Danny's presence made the situation awkward, Katherine had a hard time keeping a smile of pride from her face. "This is Mr. Dark, Mike. He's here on business. I think you should go and wait for Aunt Vic."

"Oh. Sorry." The excitement died out of the boy's voice, as his mouth crinkled into a serious frown. "Dark? Like in Dark River? Did they name Dark River after you?"

"Good question, Mike. That's exactly what I'm here to learn. The Darks were always the outcasts in town. But I came back to Dark River to set the record straight."

"That's really why you're here?" Katherine couldn't conceal a sigh of relief.

"Yes." Danny couldn't help but be aware of the change in Katherine's voice.

"How are you going to do that?" Mike asked enthusiastically.

Danny stood and allowed a smile for the boy to wash across his face. "Well, Mike, is it? Call me Danny, since Katherine seems to prefer it. Nobody really knows how the river got its name. When I was your age, my father told me that his ancestor founded the town. But nobody ever believed him. I'm going to find out the truth."

"Hey, that's neat, Danny. If you'd like to see the war game down at the barbershop, I'll show you."

"I'd like that very much, Mike," Danny said, almost certain from her expression that Katherine was upset about Mike's suggestion. He was sure of it when she spoke again.

"Mike, I don't think you should call Mr. Dark by his first name. It's not polite. Why don't you wait for Aunt Vic in the park?"

The boy pressed his lips together stubbornly for a moment before he finally held out his hand. "I'm sorry, Mr. Dark. I'll be in the park, Katherine," he said on his way out.

"Katherine? I'm Mr. Dark, but you're Katherine?" Could Mike be the source of Katherine's trouble?

"Yes, well, our relationship is different. I apologize for the interruption. I didn't intend for you to meet Mike just yet."

"Oh? Why?"

"Because I was afraid that . . . that you wouldn't understand. I mean he isn't sure of himself yet. His parents were killed in an automobile accident just six months ago. He's still settling in."

His parents? Then the boy wasn't Katherine's child. That would explain Mike's use of Katherine's name. "He's living with you and Aunt Vic?"

"Yes, I was . . . very close to his mother. Mike had no other relatives."

Katherine let out a ragged breath. Being secretive had gotten her into this trouble in the first place. Danny Dark was Mike's father. He should know. Ten years earlier she would have been honest. But Danny had disappeared. Now he'd returned, and she wasn't prepared for that much honesty until she had some answers. The risk was too great. Danny couldn't be allowed to claim

Mike before she made her own claim official. She had lost Mike once. She wasn't going to take a chance on losing him again.

"So, Mike is alone—like I was," Dan said in a strained voice, then noticed that the grimace on Katherine's face slid into a caring smile. He'd seen that smile of comfort before, through most of his growing years. Behind every door he'd slammed and every angry gesture he'd made, Katherine had been there, understanding, ready to fight off the cruelty of those who'd put him down. And now she was doing it again, defending another boy who was alone.

Her answer was a tight, "Yes."

Dan gave a quick nod. "You always did pick the underdogs. I haven't forgotten how hard it was—still is. Do you plan to raise him by yourself?"

The lump in Katherine's throat swelled and tightened. Her control was already stretched to the limit. Seeing Danny again had been enough to throw her emotions into a state of chaos, but seeing him with his son and not being able to tell him the truth was more than she could handle.

"Yes." Her answer hung between them like lead in the air. It plummeted through the silence like the sound of the church bell on a snowy night, reverberating solemnly and deeply.

Danny let out a deep breath, settling the quicksand bubbles of unease in his belly. For a moment the thought had flashed through his mind that Mike was just about the right age to have belonged to them—if things had been different. And for a moment he was sorry.

"Mike's lucky to have you," he said.

Abruptly Katherine stood and walked to the window overlooking the town square. Only she and Aunt Vic knew how lucky *she* was. She could see Mike chasing the pigeons around the statue of General Samuel Sinclair, the man who had been given credit for the founding of Dark River, the man for whom her father was named.

She heard Danny come to his feet and walk over to stand beside her. Danny was wrong. Mike wasn't alone. His adoptive parents were dead. But his real parents, both of them, were standing side by side watching him race about the tree-shaded square. Except they weren't together. Katherine felt an ache throb through her body, and it was all she could do to keep from sliding her arm around Danny's waist.

Both she and Danny had grown up without mothers. There'd been a time when she'd shared Danny's lonely pain, now she was coping with his son's. Nobody knew better than she how alone a child could be made to feel. She'd never let Mike feel abandoned and alone.

"We're only just getting to know each other," Katherine admitted. "But he seems to be adjusting to the loss of his family."

"I'm sorry, Katherine. It must be very hard for Mike. How old is he?"

Katherine felt her heart lurch in her chest. "He's nine."

"I see." He watched as Mike raced across the park green. "It's going to be hard, raising him without a father. We both know how it feels to face the future by yourself. I guess we're still doing that, aren't we?"

"Maybe, but as adults we're better prepared for living alone. A child needs a mother."

"Children can get along without one. We did. But then, I was lucky. I had someone as a child that you didn't, someone who Mike has too. And that will make all the difference in the world."

"Oh, who?"

"I had you."

It took every ounce of her self-control for Katherine to turn and face Danny. She even managed to conjure up a weak smile. Everything that had happened since the day before had been a shock to her system, an insidious shock that had begun chewing at the sturdy structure she'd built of her life. Now she felt the foundations shiver as if she were standing in a strong wind.

She had to bring this meeting to a close before she was swept away by her churning emotions. Danny—Mike—the past and the present were slamming into each other with all the force of a sandstorm in the desert, and she was caught up in the maelstrom.

"Yes," she said in a low voice. "We had each other, Danny. We were friends who supplied the support the other needed. But I . . . I'm sorry I . . . I have a luncheon with the Jaycees in fifteen minutes. Please tell me what you need from me."

"I don't think I can. Fifteen minutes isn't enough time, Katherine. My needs are a bit more complicated than that."

"Try, Danny." Katherine's throat tightened. She

had to get away. Being alone with Danny was tearing her apart. She'd thought she could be strong. But seeing him again brought back memories she couldn't, wouldn't deal with a second time.

Danny didn't answer. He just stared at her, his eyes filled with a sadness that seemed out of place. There was no reason for him to be hurt. She hadn't deserted him. She hadn't ripped his life apart and changed it forever, leaving him to face the kind of guilt a seventeen-year-old should never have to deal with.

"For some time I've had it in mind to buy the old Dark family property, Katherine. Since I have a little break before I have to begin my next project, I decided I'd come back and find out whether or not the stories my father used to brag about are true."

Build a permanent home here? Danny was actually contemplating returning to Dark River to live? Katherine hadn't known what Danny would say, but this idea had never occurred to her. She grasped at a safe comment. "What stories, Danny?"

"Surely you remember my father's drunken ramblings, that most of the town really belongs to the Darks."

Katherine couldn't stop a sad grimace. "Dark River belongs to you? Oh, Danny. You know that was only bragging for your benefit. Don't do this to yourself. You can probably buy any land you want in the area without that old story."

"You're right, I can. It's the Dark family history

I'm interested in. I have to know where I've been before I can plan the future."

Katherine felt a shiver of apprehension zigzag down her backbone. There was an ominous undertone in Danny's voice, a desperation she'd hoped he'd put behind him. His great need to be somebody had always made Danny seem stiff and unyielding. The need was still there.

"Why, Danny? What difference can the past make to you now? You don't need it."

"But I do. I guess I always have."

"So, what can I do to help?" She turned back to her desk and picked up a notepad and a pencil.

"Well, for starters, you still live in your family home, don't you?"

"Of course. When Father died, Aunt Victoria moved from the guest house into the big house with me."

Danny smiled, the first real smile of warmth Katherine had seen on his face. "Aunt Vic. She must be ninety years old."

"Seventy-eight, but don't let her know I told you. Why would you care about my house?" The pencil, which she'd held poised to take notes, had begun to make meaningless scribbles around the margins of the tablet.

"According to the town librarian, your great-grandfather had a library where he stored all the initial town council minutes."

"I think so, though I've never read them. The original secretary was married to one of the Sinclairs. When the town library was built, Father refused to give the records up. You know how he insisted on controlling everything."

"Yes, I know about that all right. I'd like to look at the minutes, Katherine. Is that possible?"

She stopped her scribbling and looked up in surprise. "What on earth do you expect to learn, Danny?"

"Everybody always assumed that the original Darks were refugees from the English prisons and that they took their name from the river. Every time my father got drunk, he swore it was the other way around. I want to prove that Dark River was named for the Dark family."

Coming back to Dark River had always been at the back of his mind. Coming back as a successful, wealthy businessman had spurred him through the worst times of his life. He'd made that dream come true. But he couldn't come back and face Katherine as he'd thought. His guilt over having left her without saying good-bye was the only part of his past he hadn't learned to deal with.

He'd found one reason after another to delay returning, until Aunt Vic had called and said that Katherine needed him. No, Aunt Vic hadn't explained why. She'd said only that he needed to come. And he had. He thought that he'd come because he owed her something. Katherine didn't know it yet, but he'd been fooling himself. He might have come back for Katherine, but he was going to stay for himself.

"Why do you care, Danny? The past is past and

we . . . you can't change that, even if you wanted to."

"Maybe you're wrong, Katherine. Maybe you've never met a man determined to try. The world may never know the truth, but I need to know that some part of Dark River belongs to me."

"But what if it doesn't?"

"That's simple. I'll buy it."

Two

After Danny left, Katherine looked down at the notepad she'd been scribbling on.

The words "Run Away! Run Away! Run Away!" were scrawled in dark, agitated letters on the yellow memo sheet. The letters stared back at her, belying any pretension she might have had at immunity to Danny's powerful presence. She crumpled the paper, flung it into the wastepaper can, and walked to the window.

She watched Danny leave her building and climb into a red convertible. He might have feared calling attention to himself before the town once, but this Danny Dark was announcing his presence in neon colors.

Danny called Mike over to the car for a moment, listening intently as the boy answered whatever his question was, then he ruffled Mike's hair affectionately. Mike nodded, glanced up at Katherine's window and grinned. He turned back to Danny as if the two had just shared a secret. Even from a distance Katherine could see how easily they responded to each other.

But Danny was easy to respond to. Her shortness of breath and scattered thoughts were proof of that.

After ten minutes of pacing her small office, she retrieved the sheet of memo paper and dropped it into her handbag, into the same compartment where Danny's letter had been stuffed, and left the office. Katherine had a date with twenty-five Jaycees for steak and french fries.

The first person to tell her that Danny Dark was back in town was her old friend Joe Hall, who ran the Dark River Inn where the Jaycees met. He intercepted Katherine as she stepped up on the veranda.

"Hey, Kakki, have you heard that Danny is back?"

"Yes. He came by my office this morning. How did you know?"

"He's staying here."

Katherine came to a stop, catching the back of the huge rocking chair beside her. Without being obvious she glanced around. The last thing she needed right now was another meeting with Danny. She hadn't had time to get past their first, and she certainly hadn't come to terms with his presence in town.

"Here?"

"Don't worry, kid," Joe said with a knowing smile. "He isn't here now. He left about an hour ago and hasn't come back. Are you going to be all right?"

"Certainly I'm all right, Joe!" Katherine realized she was snapping at her dearest friend. And she knew it was obvious to Joe that she wasn't all right.

"You aren't fooling me, kid. Slip in through the back door with me, and I'll fix you something to reinforce that suit of professional armor you usually carry around."

Numbly Katherine followed Joe. She was grateful he didn't ask questions. But Joe never had. He'd been there more than once when she'd needed a shoulder to cry on. It had been Joe, the big, lovable, gruff-talking football player, who had been Katherine's official escort for years—off to the homecoming dance and drop Katherine by the river to meet Danny afterward; pick her up for play practice and disappear while she and Danny sat in the shadows and talked. He'd never complained about Katherine's choosing Danny over him then, and he was prepared to be her protector now, too, if that was what she needed.

When Joe mixed up a glass of fruit juice and handed it to her, Katherine dutifully took a sip and swallowed with a choking gulp. "Joe! That's pretty strong reinforcement."

"You looked like you needed something strong. What does he want, Katherine?"

"Believe it or not, he wants to buy Dark River."

"The town?"

"That's what he said."

"Well, from what I've heard about him, he can probably do it."

"Oh? What have you heard?" Katherine took

another big swallow of her juice and silently thanked Joe for the warm glow that was beginning to seep through her body.

"Well, you know from the newspaper stories that he's joined the ranks of the rich and famous. He's the owner of a firm that acts as a go-between for the big money investors and folks who need funds invested in their projects. For a nice slice of the profits, of course. And I'm told that he makes plenty of that. His latest project is a hydroelectric plant in Saudi Arabia."

She took another sip of her drink. "I never expected him to come back after so long."

"Does seem odd that he's come now. How are you getting on with your young relative?"

"Mike? Fine. You know Aunt Vic, she could make Genghis Khan feel at home."

"Kakki, you know, it's none of my business, but I think we've been good enough friends for me to say what's on my mind."

"Of course we are, Joe."

"Well, you may have the town convinced the kid is some distant relative, but I think he's a lot closer to you, isn't he?"

"Is it so obvious?"

"That he looks like you? Yes. That he's your child? No."

Katherine felt her heart stop for an uneven second. "You knew?"

"Let's just say I suspected. Is that why Danny's here?"

"No. Danny doesn't know anything. Neither does Mike—yet. I haven't told him. I wanted to give him a chance to feel comfortable before he learned the truth. Now, I don't know."

The sound of laughter from the private dining room beyond grew in intensity as the Jaycees began to gather. Joe's hotel was the only establishment of its kind in town. The Dark River City Council zealously protected their little town from outside commerce. They liked it just as it was, and they intended to do everything they could to maintain the status quo.

Katherine knew it wouldn't do for the mayor to arrive late, so she buoyed herself up and attended the luncheon.

As she was driving home, she thought about Joe.

Dear Joe. Why couldn't she have fallen for him ten years before? Why wasn't it him she was thinking of now? She knew he'd always cared for her, and her father had approved of Joe.

Katherine smiled. Her father wouldn't have believed that it was Danny who had gone on to become wealthy and Joe who'd stayed in Dark River to become an innkeeper. So much for her father's judgment. Sam Sinclair was gone, but Katherine could still feel his censure where Danny was concerned.

The office of mayor was only part-time and Katherine's hours were of her own making. At home, after attempting to do some consulting work, she abandoned the idea in favor of a mean game of blackjack with Mike. Later she tried to take a nap, but she never closed her eyes. Finally giving up, she took a shower and went downstairs to face Aunt Vic. But Victoria was uncharacteristically silent, puttering around the kitchen as though she were preoccupied with preparing the evening meal.

Katherine might have questioned her aunt's silence if she hadn't been so involved with her own thoughts. As she set the table for supper she was still trying to decide whether or not she could keep the meeting with Danny from Aunt Vic.

Katherine didn't know how to explain the new misgivings she had about concealing the truth from Danny. She didn't know how she would deal with Danny's plan to learn the truth about his past.

Finally she said, "Danny came to my office today. He wants to use our library, Aunt Vic. That's why he came back."

"I know. Mike told me. What did you say?"

"I don't think I ever said anything. But he has a way of getting what he wants. Maybe the quicker he finds what he's looking for, the quicker he'll be gone."

"I'm sure you're right."

"I suppose I'll have to allow it. I'll call him."

"That won't be necessary, Katherine dear. I knew you'd make the proper decision. He'll be here any minute."

Katherine Sinclair felt the knife she was holding fall from her fingers to drop on the table with a thud. She looked up in shock at the pixie-faced woman stirring the pot on the stove. "What do you mean, he'll be here any minute?"

"I told him you'd probably offer to let him stay in the guest cottage. It needs a little airing out, but it'll be a good way for Danny and Mike to get to know each other."

"No! I don't want him to get to know Mike, Aunt Vic. Don't you see, what if he wants to take Mike?"

Aunt Vic always had a mind of her own, but it was unlike her to offer Danny the guest house without discussing it.

"Oh, Katherine, I'm sorry if I did the wrong thing. When he called this afternoon and told me what he was trying to do, I didn't have the heart to tell him no. Mike is the only family Danny has left, and Danny needs a family. That's why he's on this wild-goose chase about Dark River."

"Are you sure it isn't because of Mike that he came?"

"I'm sure, Katherine."

A sense of foreboding came over Katherine. Warily she looked up at Aunt Vic. "How do you know that?"

"Because I . . . I sent for Danny, Katherine. I didn't tell him anything else. I just told him it was time he came home. In fact . . ."

"In fact, what? I'm afraid to ask."

"You'd better set another place. I invited him for dinner."

"You did what?"

"He doesn't know about Mike, Katherine. That's

up to you. I simply told him that you needed him. You always have. You still do."

This time the fork didn't land on the table. It slipped through Katherine's fingers and clattered to the floor.

"We're having pot roast." Victoria went on seemingly oblivious to her niece's astonishment. "With corn on the cob and green beans."

The elderly woman lifted her spoon from the pot and blew on the liquid it held. After several cooling breaths she tasted it.

"Needs more salt."

"You sent for Danny? I didn't even know where he was. How did you find him?"

"Anybody could have found him, what with his name being in the newspaper almost every day. Joe checked it out for me. It wasn't hard."

"It wasn't hard?" Katherine couldn't even think. When she'd needed Danny, she'd looked, with no results. Then, after she'd stopped looking, finding Danny turned out to be easy. Now, after years of learning to live without her child and the man she'd loved, both of them had come abruptly back into her life. Mike was a joyous gift, a second chance. But Danny? She didn't know how she felt about him.

"He had ten years to come back, Aunt Vic, and he didn't. Then you call, and he responds immediately. Why? What exactly did you tell him?"

"I just said that you needed him."

"Well, I don't. Not anymore. And I don't want him to know about Mike yet. I won't let Danny interfere. Where is Mike?"

Katherine knew she was overreacting. She just couldn't seem to get her emotions under control.

"Washing up. Do you really think he would? Danny, of all people, wouldn't want to separate a child from his mother. He knows what it's like not to have a mother. What you've got to decide is whether or not you want Mike to grow up without a father. Or haven't you thought about that?"

"I haven't thought about anything else since I opened that note. But I don't have any answers, and I don't think I can sit across the table from Danny until I've decided how I feel. Make an excuse for me, Aunt Vic, because I'm not going to be here."

Katherine gave a swift kick to the fork, sending it skidding under the table. She whirled around, marching out of the kitchen and onto the porch.

If she'd been five minutes sooner, she would have made it. If Danny had had the manners Aunt Vic had attributed to him, he would have gone to the front door instead of the porch.

"Hi, Mr. Dark." Mike ran through the kitchen behind Katherine. "Come on in. Isn't this some house?"

"Yes, it is, Mike. I'm very impressed. Southfork in Southern Georgia."

Katherine could only stand there with her mouth open.

"I'll bet where you live is something too," Aunt Vic said with a laugh from the kitchen. "Come on in, Danny. This does look something like Southfork, doesn't it? Except we don't have any cattle, and we don't have a cook and a maid. There's just me and a cleaning lady who comes twice a week. Pick up that fork under the table, will you, Mike?"

"I'm sorry, Katherine," Danny said. "I see that you weren't expecting me. Would you rather I leave?"

Katherine let her shoulders sag in defeat. "Please come in. Aunt Vic invited you. What I would have preferred isn't important." She stared stoically at the man in the shadows. She knew she sounded peevish, but she couldn't seem to stop herself.

When Danny stepped inside, Katherine felt her stomach muscles contract and she knew she'd made a mistake. He'd exchanged his jacket and cotton slacks for blue jeans, sport shirt, and sneakers.

The man in her office had been Dan Dark—confident, successful, determined. The man standing before her was the Danny of the past. Leaning against the door frame, arms crossed over his chest, a defiant expression on his face, he looked like his son had earlier in her office.

Danny had never been inside her house before, and she knew without his saying it that he wasn't over that rejection, no matter how jaunty he tried to appear. This was the boy she'd befriended in the third grade and would love for the rest of her life; the wary, uncertain boy who'd always had her in his corner.

He said softly, "Your preference is the only one that does count."

She believed him. "Come in, Danny. You're welcome here."

"We both know that isn't true, Katherine, but I'm working on changing that."

"Hey, Mr. Dark, Aunt Vic has made banana pudding for dessert. And the tomatoes are out of her garden. And she has a new video game. This is a neat place for two guys like us."

"Two guys like us?" Katherine repeated Mike's casual statement.

"Aunt Vic says that Mr. Dark is going to stay here for a few days. I think that's neat."

Katherine didn't believe that her home was a "neat" place for kids. But she was willing to concede that her opinion was biased. Living in this house after her mother died was the reason she had understood Danny's unhappiness so well. And until her father's death, when Aunt Vic had moved from the guest house into the main house, the place had seemed filled with rules and punishments. But Aunt Vic had changed all that.

Aunt Vic had always liked Danny. She'd never made a secret of it. Whenever she'd taken Katherine to Savannah to the museum, to the amusement park, to the symphony, she'd always included the scruffy, sullen boy.

That Katherine's father was never a party to their secret trips wasn't discussed. If he'd asked, Victoria would have answered honestly, without fear. But he never had. As long as Katherine had maintained the proper Sinclair image, her father had been pleased.

In junior high Danny had begun to believe that he was a threat to Katherine's image. She'd argued that she didn't care. Still, even then she'd understood that any trouble Danny got into had been his shield against the pain. His father's reputation had smeared Danny with the kind of stigma he couldn't counteract.

There were times, later, when Danny had become so angry that he'd allowed himself to take advantage of his reputation. But he hadn't been guilty of stealing the chemistry exams—one of many offenses attributed to him. He hadn't needed the tests to make high grades. And the drugs found in his high school locker weren't his, but nobody ever considered that they'd been stashed there in order to protect the real pusher. There were other things, things he'd never told Katherine, things she learned from others.

Katherine had always believed in Danny, and he'd needed that trust. Danny had said that if the Dark family hadn't been in the area first, they'd never have been allowed to live in the small bedroom community outside Savannah, Georgia.

So they kept secret their friendship, then later their love for each other. No one knew except Joe and Aunt Vic, though it was never openly discussed. In the years since, Katherine realized that hiding their feelings from the world had made them all the more intense.

Explosive.

Wonderful.

Disastrous.

Now Danny was back and all those feelings were free to surface again. But this time Katherine wouldn't allow herself to be swept up in Danny's spell. What happened would be her choice, not Danny's. Katherine Sinclair wasn't afraid anymore.

"Danny, I don't think any of this is a good idea. I don't believe that it's in Mike's best interest for you to be here. He likes you, and he's vulnerable right now. After losing his parents, I don't want him to come to depend on you. You'll just move on."

"I agree," Danny said softly. "And I promise that I won't do anything to cause you or Mike pain. What happens is up to you."

"If I really thought you meant that . . . All right, you can go through the records—for a month. There's only one condition."

"Oh? What's that?"

"The arrangement is business—not personal."

"Are you sure, Katherine?"

"I'm sure, Danny."

Katherine seemed surprised at how smoothly dinner went. Aunt Vic and Danny kept up a steady stream of conversation. Danny didn't find it at all hard to believe that Aunt Vic really played video games and had her own private supply in her study. But he turned down the invitation she and Mike issued to challenge them after they finished the dishes.

Despite her decision to allow Danny access to her library, Katherine still hadn't made up her mind whether she could accept Danny's presence in her house. There was a tenseness in her stomach that grew tighter and tighter in stubborn resistance. No matter how brave she pretended to be, she was disturbed.

Even without Mike's presence, their relationship was different now. The trust was gone. And trust was the basis of friendship. No matter what kind of signals her body was sending, she'd changed and so had Danny.

From the time he'd entered the house, every glance, every recalled incident, was almost a physical linking between them. And she didn't want to feel the connection. It was too much, too soon. She needed time to think and to get her emotions under control. Across the table, Danny was questioning Mike about school.

"Are you a good student?"

"Nah. I don't much like school."

"Neither did I," agreed Danny.

"I don't understand it," Aunt Vic observed. "You were a good student, Danny. I remember once when we were in the museum, you could name every prehistoric creature there."

"Just like my dad," Mike agreed. "He was pretty smart, too, but he didn't care much about grades. As long as I stayed out of trouble, that's all he was interested in. He didn't expect me to be a brain. But Katherine, well, she treats me like my mom did."

Katherine sat up sharply. "I only want you to do your best," she said with a smile.

"My mom and pop were in an automobile accident," Mike explained. "They weren't my real parents," Mike said in a low voice. "I . . . I was adopted. My real mother couldn't take care of me.

Then my grandmother got sick and she had to call that lawyer to find a new home for me. He said that Katherine was a friend of my mother's. She came and brought me home."

Danny didn't know whether the quick breath he heard came from Katherine, her aunt, or himself.

But it was Katherine who looked stricken. Her face was as white as new snow. "I didn't know that you knew you were adopted, darling. Why didn't you tell me?"

"Mom said it was a secret. That I shouldn't tell. Then I was afraid that you'd send me back, too."

"When did you find out, Mike?" Aunt Vic asked softly.

"They told me when I was a little kid. I just don't know why my real mother gave me away. But Granny said I should be good for Katherine. And I really like it here."

This time it was Danny who dropped the silverware.

"Mike, my love," Aunt Vic said, sliding him into her lap. "Your mother and father loved you very much. I believe that with all my heart. And I want you to believe that, too."

But this time Mike didn't answer. Instead he burrowed his head against Aunt Vic's shoulder and choked back a sob.

As if she were sleepwalking Katherine stood, walked out on the porch and into the garden.

She should have known that Danny would follow. He'd always been there for her—except once. But this was different. Because of Danny she'd given up a part of her life. Now she'd gotten it back. But what would Mike say when he learned that she had been the one who'd given him away?

Behind her in the kitchen she could hear Aunt Vic's quiet voice. She was probably still holding Mike in her arms just as she'd comforted Katherine as a child. It ought to be her job to comfort Mike, but instead she had to face Danny. There was no more time for secrets. No matter what the outcome was, she had to tell him the truth.

Danny would soon know what had happened, if he didn't already. Maybe what he'd really come back for was revenge.

"You're Mike's mother, aren't you, Katherine?"

"Yes."

"I don't understand," he said softly.

Katherine was a strong woman, a woman who wouldn't cry. She kept telling herself that she'd already cried too many tears. A wall of pain welled up in her throat, and she couldn't answer. It still hurt too much.

After a long silence, Danny spoke again. "Is—is Mike my son?"

The question had come, and she couldn't lie. She simply nodded.

Behind her, Danny took a deep breath. There was a long, painful moment of silence before he asked the question she expected. "Why, why did you give up our child, Katherine?"

She swallowed hard, forcing open the passageway so that she could speak. She wouldn't break. She'd let years of resentment and anger carry her through the pain. It was because of Danny that she'd had to make such a desperate decision. If only he'd been there . . .

"How can you even ask me that? Where were you when I needed you? Why didn't you meet me that last night after graduation, Danny?"

"I . . . I couldn't." It was Danny's voice that was hoarse now. "Something happened. I wanted to be there, but I had no choice in what I did."

"Neither did I, Danny."

"Tell me the way it was, Katherine. Spell it out. I could understand if you'd had an abortion. You were scared. I wouldn't have liked it, but I'd have understood."

"An abortion? You think I could have considered such a thing? The baby was ours. I loved you, Danny. Abortion? No!" The thought caused a sharp pain in her chest.

"Could it have been any worse than what you did?" He knew he was being cruel. He hated himself for it, knowing he could have prevented what had happened. But the past was the past, and he couldn't change it now. How Katherine felt about what had happened and what she felt about Mike was what mattered.

"I was seventeen years old. You're right, I was scared out of my mind to face my father. And I didn't know where you were. I thought you'd left me. I was alone. You probably can't understand that."

"Yes, I can, Katherine. I understand it better than you think. I've lived with what I did every lonely night since. I should have been there for you. I would have, if I'd known." He sighed.

"We've both suffered for our mistakes, haven't we? At least you had Aunt Vic."

"Yes, and you had a father, too. But you left him. Even he didn't know where you were."

"He didn't want to. He never cared anything about me. He made my life hell."

"Which was exactly what my father would have done to our child. I loved him, even then, too much to bring him into my father's house. Don't you see? Neither of us had a mother. A child deserves a mother and a father. I wanted what was best for the baby—a real family, a home."

Danny's breath came in ragged gulps as he allowed her words to fill his mind. "Then you didn't give our son away because you didn't want him?"

"Oh, Danny, of course not." She moaned softly, trying desperately to hold back the dam of hot tears threatening to spill over at any moment. "I gave him up because I loved him so very much."

She was grateful that he'd remained in the darkness behind her. She wasn't sure she could have met the accusation in his eyes. What could they say to each other to justify the decisions they'd made?

It was Danny who hadn't kept their last meeting, when she would have told him about the child. It was Danny who'd disappeared. And now it was time for his truth, too.

"Where were you, Danny? Why didn't you come? I need to know."

"All right. It doesn't matter anymore, I guess. I got a call from a friend, somebody who needed help over in Brooks County. I went, and walked into a setup."

"What do you mean, a setup? What friend?"

"There was a guy I knew, a man I'd asked a few favors from. His car had broken down. He asked me to go over, get it running, and bring it back. The Brooks police stopped me, accused me of car theft, and put me in jail. They wouldn't even allow me a phone call."

"You were in jail?"

"I was in jail for three days before they finally released me. By that time it was made painfully clear that if I ever saw you again, I'd spend a much longer time in a jail that wouldn't be nearly as comfortable."

"But, Danny, you weren't a car thief. You were only seventeen. Surely it was a mistake."

"I was old enough to be tried as an adult. Car theft, on top of the other things I'd already done, put me in big trouble, Katherine."

"Oh, Danny, I still don't understand. Why didn't you call me?"

"I did. But your father wouldn't let me talk to you. I called my dad, but wouldn't you know? It was one of those times when he'd suddenly come into some money, and he was gone, too. I was on my own, and I didn't have any choice. Either I left town, or I went to jail."

"So you left."

"I left. I thought I didn't have a choice."

"But later? You could have come back later. It's been ten years, Danny."

"Later? I did, but you were gone. He planned it all very carefully."

"He?"

There was a long silence.

"Your father."

"My father?"

Suddenly she understood. "Oh, Danny. It was my father who set you up? He knew how much I loved you, and he sent you away. I'm so sorry."

"He's not entirely to blame, Katherine. The truth is, I guess I let him. I finally realized that the way I was going, I would never have anything to offer you. It was better if I disappeared, at least until I'd made something of myself."

"That isn't true, Danny. I always knew what you were."

"No, you knew what you wanted me to be. I'm not proud of what I was or what I did. I let him buy me off with a college education. I traded success for the woman I loved—and the child I never knew about. I was too ashamed to face you."

There was nothing Katherine could say. She knew about shame and guilt. She'd lived with them both. And for ten years she'd believed that Danny had deserted her. Now she'd learned that her father had forced him to go.

"I'm sorry, Katherine, truly," Danny said roughly. "What would have happened if I'd come that night?"

At last Katherine turned to face him. She took a deep, shaky breath and answered. "I'd have told you that I was pregnant."

"And then what, Katherine?" Danny forced

himself to play out the scene as unemotionally as it was possible to do. "We would have gotten married?"

"That's what I wanted, more than anything in the world, Danny," she said simply.

"You know it wouldn't have worked. I was a kid, barely able to take care of myself. There is no way we would have survived if we'd married each other then. Your father and this town would have beaten us before we got started."

"Yes. I see that now."

"What did you do, Katherine? How did you get through having a child alone?"

"I wasn't alone. Aunt Vic was with me. After I decided that you weren't coming back, we went to Europe. When Aunt Vic found out that I was pregnant, we came back here long enough to meet with an attorney who specialized in private adoptions. He let me choose the parents. Then I went away to have Mike."

"Did you hate me for what you had to go through alone?"

"Hate you? Yes, for a while. Then when I felt him move . . . Oh, Danny, they took him away. I never even held him. Afterward, I entered college, and nobody ever knew."

Katherine's words were tight and strained. Listening to her, Danny knew she deliberately hadn't told him how hard it had been. She'd left out a lot, just as he had. Katherine was too kind and loving to have borne all that without going through some kind of hell. He felt hot tears behind his eyelids, and he knew that for all the bad times he'd experienced, he'd had it easy compared to Katherine.

All he wanted to do was pull her into his arms and say how sorry he was. But he didn't. She was trying so hard to be strong, and he knew that with one touch they'd both fall apart.

"The adoptive parents," he went on, pulling out all the details as if by knowing he could find some solace, "were they good people?"

"Yes, I think so." Katherine forced herself to answer. It had to be said, once and for all time. "I made the attorney find out everything about them. For weeks I read and thought and . . ."

"Agonized," he finished her sentence for her.

"Yes. Making a choice was the most difficult thing I had to do. I wanted so badly for our child to have two parents, two loving parents who would give him the kind of life neither one of us had."

"Yes."

"I liked it that the man was an ordinary person, owned a hardware store. There was something stable about that. His wife was a nursery-school teacher. She would understand children. I knew everything about them except their names and where they lived. They kept that information from me."

The moon slipped from behind a cloud, throwing a silvery cast across the garden. At last Danny could see her face, as white as her hair in the moonlight. He stepped closer, then winced when she automatically moved away.

Danny knew now why Aunt Vic had sent for

him. He had the truth about the past, but the truth brought only anger and frustration. Katherine had done what she'd thought was right for Mike. And she'd lived with her decision ever since. But now he knew he had a child, a child she'd denied him.

Mike was his son.

Katherine, the woman he'd loved for most of his life, had borne his child, in secret, alone. As he noted the uncertainty in her eyes Danny felt his anger drain away. Katherine was hurting, too. Instead of pressuring her into defending her actions, he should be comforting her. They should be comforting each other.

"Aunt Vic knew about me, didn't she?"

"She never asked who the father was, and I never told her. But she had to have guessed. Oh, Danny, I could have lived in peace with any part of what happened if they'd let me see him—just once." She choked back a sob and bent her head to get away from the sympathy in his eyes.

"I should have been there when you needed me, Katherine. You were always there for me. Maybe it's too late to make that up to you, but I'm here now. And I'm going to stay for as long as I can for both of you."

When his arms went around her, it seemed right. Katherine closed her eyes for a moment, trying to erase the anguish she'd heard in Danny's voice. She felt his hand slide up her shoulders and his fingers thread through her hair. Then the reality of his words hit her. "As long as you can? What does that mean?"

"It means . . ." he tried to put his answer in some kind of honest perspective as the smell of her teased his senses. "It means that I have a business to run, Katherine. A business that requires my covering a good part of the world from time to time. I have to be in Saudi Arabia next month and in Brazil the month afterward. But I'll be back this time, I promise."

She tensed. "I see. You become part of our lives and drop in from time to time to check on our well-being?"

"What happens now is what you and I have to decide."

Katherine unclasped her hands from behind his back and let them fall to her sides, tilting her head back so that she could see his face. "What are you offering, Danny?"

Danny's arms tightened around her waist.

"I'm not sure. I came back because you needed me. But I'm tired of wandering, Katherine, tired of being alone."

It was so bright in the moonlight. She couldn't mistake the passion in his eyes, but there was pain, too, pain that took her back to the river and their time together so long ago. She didn't want to remember. She didn't want to feel. Their need for each other wasn't the important thing anymore.

"Maybe we ought to get married, and tell Mike the truth."

Three

The garden was silent.

The moon vanished behind a cloud.

Katherine gave a confused moan. She took a deep breath, trying to separate her thoughts. She had a great need to believe Danny's words, to allow herself, just for a moment to feel the warmth and comfort of his arms.

"No, Danny." Katherine forced herself to pull back. "No. It isn't that simple. We can't go back and take up where we left off. What we have to do now is decide what's best for Mike."

"It's Mike I'm thinking of. He's just lost two people who loved him, but he was wrong about one thing. His real mother and father were two seventeen-year-olds who were crazy in love and too young to know how to hold on to what they had. We're grown-up now, Katherine, and I intend to hold on to what's mine."

"Legally Mike is my son —not yours."

"I see."

Danny felt the cold calm of Katherine's rejection sweep over him. He turned away, walking deeper into the garden. He acknowledged to himself that it hurt to know he had never been told about his child. He could understand Katherine's not being able to find him when Mike was born, but she could have reached him later. She should have known how much it would mean to him to know he had a son. He was Mike's father.

The fact that she hadn't contacted him when she got the message from the attorney was an overt rejection he was having a hard time dealing with.

"No, he's our son," Danny said with a low moan.

"Our son," she echoed. Just saying the words changed everything. The realization came tumbling out, free and clear. She could finally allow herself to speak the truth.

"Yes. I'm his mother. Mike is my son. Mike is a part of me, a part that has been missing. But Danny, he *is* your son, too." The last wall around her heart came tumbling down. The tears slid freely down her cheeks.

"Oh, Danny, I'm so sorry," she whispered, "for both of us. We've lost so much that was precious."

Danny turned. He couldn't see her face in the darkness. But he didn't have to. He'd seen her tears and felt her heartache before. He felt it again now. "So am I, Katherine. I should have been there for you. I'm here now."

"For how long?"

"I don't know. I've worked hard to become successful, respectable. Surely you understand that. I can't just walk away and leave it."

"I do understand, Danny. And I want you to be here, and that scares me. But if you're going to make me love you and leave again, I can't take that—and neither can Mike."

"Ah, Katherine, I'd like to promise you that I won't have to leave you ever again. But I can't. What I will promise is that I'll never deliberately hurt you again. Are you going to let me tell Mike—" this time his voice broke, "I'm his father?"

"That choice will have to be yours, Danny. The only thing I insist on is that you first let me tell him I'm his mother."

"And when will that be, Katherine?"

"I don't know. When I think he's ready. Mike's a good kid. Right now he's still pretty confused. I'm still not sure your being here is a good idea, certainly not if it's only going to be temporary."

Danny couldn't hold back any longer. For all the years he'd been gone, he'd dreamed about this woman, unconsciously loved her with every step he'd taken toward respectability, looked for her in every woman he'd left behind along the way. There was no way he could do this logically or unemotionally. She was too important. Without thinking he stepped forward and slid his arms around her, clasping her close with a groan that expressed better than words the emotional turmoil he was feeling.

A shudder ripped through him, setting off a matching shiver in the woman pressing softly against his chest.

"I think my being here is a very good idea. I

think I'm still in love with you, Katherine. And I don't want to lose either you or Mike again."

"Please don't do this, Danny. What we were to each other is past. I don't even know how I feel about you, and I'm just learning to be with my child. There is no us, and I won't let there be. Even if that makes me some terrible person, I don't care."

"There's no way you could ever be anything but good. I just need to know if there is room in your life for someone else. Lord . . . I know I'm not doing this right, and the last thing I want to do is hurt you again."

He nestled his face in her hair and groaned in frustration. "The truth is, Katherine, Mike needs a father. I'd like it to be his real one."

Katherine stiffened and swore softly. "This is just what I didn't want to happen. I don't think I could take it if you came back into my life and disappeared again. A part of me died ten years ago, Danny, and I couldn't go through that again."

He waited a long time before he answered. He was afraid to say the words, but even more afraid not to. "I still care about you."

Katherine slid her hands between them and pushed herself away. She shook her head. "No, I don't want to hear that now, Danny. It's too soon. It's too late. I'm not sure either of us could ever trust the other again. We've grown up, changed, built different lives."

"But I think we still love each other, Katherine."

"No. If we feel something, it's because of Mike.

Or maybe we're both in love with the memory of being in love."

"Maybe, but neither of us has married."

"How do we know that what we feel isn't just pure lust?"

Danny grinned. This time his lips weren't drawn into a frown. "Well, now, at least, you're willing to concede that you still feel something, too."

"Yes, I suppose you know me too well for me to say otherwise, but that isn't enough. We ought to have learned something over the years."

"You're right." He turned serious again. "But we have a child borne of those memories from the past, and I think we owe it to him to give ourselves a chance to find out whether or not we belong together."

"Suppose we find out that we've lost our past, that there isn't anything there but lust?" She had to ask the question.

"I don't believe that," Danny said quietly. "The past was the only thing that kept me going for a very long time."

"Yes, but I read once that 'the past is a foreign country. They do things differently there.' You may find out you've been free too long to change."

Danny took Katherine's hands and removed them from his chest. He held them for a long minute. The moon came back out from behind the cloud and showered her with light.

She didn't realize how badly she'd wanted him to kiss her until he did.

She hadn't known how ragged her control was until she felt the warmth of his lips against hers.

All the years of restraint fell away. She couldn't breathe. It was so right to be kissing Danny, to open her lips to the taste of his tongue, to respond to his touch with soft moans of desire. She'd thought she'd forgotten how Danny felt, how he tasted, how he made her pulse race and her heart sing. But, Lordy, it was still there.

"Oh, Katherine," he murmured thickly. "I've missed you so damned much."

Katherine jerked herself back from his embrace and stood, breathing raggedly. Her mind was whirling.

"I never could stay away from you," Danny said fiercely, "even when I knew it was wrong."

"You must," she managed in a whisper. "We can't let our desire for each other decide what happens. We might hurt Mike more than we already have."

"Are you telling me that you don't want me to kiss you?"

"I think you know that isn't true, Danny, but we must not lose control. We have to make rational decisions. We gave in to our passion before. This time we have to find out whether or not we want to be together forever."

"I don't know if I can be around you and not touch you, Katherine."

"I don't know if I can be around you and not let you, Danny." Katherine took a deep breath and adjusted her blouse. "But I'm going to try. If there's one thing I have learned, it's that I can do what I have to. Right now all I want is to be Mike's mother."

Danny bit back a sigh. "Yes, and that's what you should be, but—ah, Katherine, it's selfish and I know it, but I want more."

"What, Danny?"

"I want you to be what I wouldn't let you be ten years ago. I want Katherine Sinclair to be Danny's girl."

"So, you're leaving town?" Joe Hall inserted the gold credit card into the slot and waited for the machine to approve its use.

"Not exactly," Danny answered. "If I should get any telephone calls, I can be reached at Kath—the Sinclair house."

Joe's gaze shot up. He frowned as he watched the approval number flash on the credit card machine, inserted the charge slip, and completed the transaction. "I don't quite know how to say this, Dan, but we think a great deal of Katherine. We—I wouldn't want to see her hurt again."

"I don't intend to allow that to happen, old friend," Danny said with a sigh of resignation. Under his breath he added, "if I can help it."

He'd purposefully waited until Katherine left for work before he'd driven down the long drive to the Sinclair estate. On either side of the hard-packed gravel road, a line of deep pink crape myrtles were in full bloom. Beside the house stood two magnolias as tall as office buildings, their branches dotted with fat creamy white blossoms.

At the entrance to the property Danny heard a shout and came to a stop as Mike came bursting through the hedge.

"Hi, Danny, are you moving in?"

"Sure thing. Climb in and give me a hand."

The boy vaulted over the open door of the convertible and leaned back, staring up at the lacy leaf-patterned arbor overhead.

"Are you going to have a house like this?"

"No. This house is over two hundred years old. It takes time to build character like this."

He drove around the house, past the pool, and stopped at the white clapboard guest house with the dormer windows. He was glad it wasn't a big house. Though he could and had lived pretty much where he wanted for the last years, there was something awe-inspiring about the Sinclair home. Danny still felt out of place. He wondered again whether or not this was a good idea. He hadn't intended to start out by being on the defensive, but somehow he was.

Mike was out of the car and racing toward the pool before Danny came to a full stop. "See the pool, Danny. The water's warm enough to swim in now. Hi, Aunt Vic. Danny's here. I'm going to help him move in."

"Good idea, Mike," she replied from the kitchen doorway. "Danny might like a swim afterward."

Danny considered the invitation. "Thanks, Aunt Vic, but I don't want to take advantage of your hospitality."

"The pool is part of the rental agreement. Didn't you read the fine print?" Aunt Vic said, wiping her hands on her apron as she walked out into the backyard. "And I have some juice on the counter if you're thirsty, Mike."

Danny slammed the car door and started toward Victoria. He hadn't thought this all out the previous night. He'd been so confused by the conflicting emotions that had come out of his and Katherine's meeting, he hadn't considered the full implication of what staying in the guest house would mean. He certainly hadn't considered that he'd still feel like a trespasser.

As Mike waited for him to agree Danny realized that any feeling of discomfort was only on his part. "Maybe later," he said and watched as the boy dashed across the yard and into the house.

His son. The thought still seemed unreal.

"It will be all right, Danny," Aunt Vic said.

"I don't know. It's all become so complicated," Danny admitted. "I'm not sure I ought to have come back. I may just make things harder for Katherine."

"You ought to have come back a long time ago, but you didn't. Thanks to what Katherine's father did, you didn't have a choice back then. This time you do."

Danny looked up in surprise. "You know about that?"

"I didn't find out what Sam had done until just before he died. He meant well, Dan. He only had Katherine's best interest at heart. He just never knew how to love her. And he certainly didn't know how strongly she felt about you. Later, I didn't know where you were, and the truth would only have made Katherine feel worse."

"I suppose so," Danny agreed. Aunt Vic was right. There were times when he cursed Samuel Sinclair. Now, as a father, he was beginning to understand how nothing was ever black or white.

"There's one thing I never understood," Victoria said. "Why didn't you try to reach Katherine?"

"You think I didn't? I called, well, not right away, but as soon as I'd had time to think about it. She'd already gone to Europe. Then later I tried to reach her at school. They said she wasn't there."

"She entered . . . late."

Danny swallowed hard. "I know that now. But when my letters were never answered, I thought she didn't want to see me anymore."

"I don't think she ever got them, Danny."

"I finally realized that. About five years ago I got up the nerve to try one last time. I called Joe Hall. He told me she was engaged. After that I stopped trying."

Mike dashed back toward the pool, sloshing the orange juice in the crystal glasses he was holding onto the patio. "Danny, Aunt Vic squeezed juice for you, too."

"Are you sure, Victoria?" Danny wasn't just asking about the juice, and Victoria knew it. When she nodded, Danny knew that his last barrier to the future had been dissolved.

"I'm sure, Dan. Now, you get unpacked. When you're finished, Mike and I will entertain ourselves while you start on those council minutes."

The chore of unpacking was made lighter work as Mike asked question after question about the deserts of Saudi Arabia and other places Danny told him he'd been. By the time Aunt Vic came to collect Mike, Danny had had a chance to see not only Katherine's zest for life in their son, but signs of the same kind of inquiring mind that he'd always had.

"What will it be, Mike?" Aunt Vic asked. "The pool? You want to help me in my greenhouse, or shall we play in the train garden?"

"The train garden! Definitely the trains."

Danny listened to the boy's excitement as he and Aunt Vic disappeared down the path through a shoulder-high hedge.

Other than Katherine, Victoria was the only person in Danny's life who had accepted him as an equal—just as she was doing with Mike. He had the odd feeling that time had folded over itself, repeating the pattern of his own life again.

After changing into an old pair of shorts and a faded T-shirt, Danny made his way into the house and found the library. At first he had an uneasy feeling about being in Samuel Sinclair's study. The old man's presence was so strong there. From the portrait above the fireplace his eyes seemed to follow Danny's movements with an accusing glare.

Danny forced himself to shake off the sensation of being an intruder. After all, this whole venture was for Mike. Old Sam had done his dead level best to control Katherine's life once; Danny wouldn't allow it to continue now that the man was dead. He began to pull old ledgers from the shelves, quickly discovering that they were not in any particular order. His task was proving to be more difficult than he'd imagined—in every possible way.

More than an hour had passed when Danny heard the sound of the heavy oak door opening. He looked up, half-expecting to see Victoria standing there with cookies and milk.

Instead it was Katherine who poked her head through the doorway. He wasn't surprised to feel the surge of emotion that rose inside his throat.

"Do you want some lunch?" she asked.

"Lunch?"

Katherine watched as a frown crinkled Danny's face. He was sitting in her father's chair, his bare feet propped lazily on a stack of ledger books on top of the desk.

"Yes, you are familiar with that meal that comes in the middle of the day. Aunt Vic and Mike are planning a picnic. She made extra sandwiches for us."

Danny sat up and tucked the ends of his shirt into his shorts. "I didn't expect her to feed me, Katherine. It's too much for her to take on that burden."

"You're right. I've engaged someone to help out with the cooking and shopping while you're here, and the cleaning woman is going to come three times a week instead of twice. I expect you to pay both their salaries."

"Of course, but will your aunt go along with that?"

"Oh, she'd much rather play with Mike."

"Fine," Danny agreed. "Paying a cook and housekeeper will make me feel as if I'm assuming some responsibility for my fam—son."

Katherine stepped back into the lighted hallway behind her. The sight of Danny in those shorts affected her more than she expected. Simply existing in the same space with him caused excitement her body didn't need.

For years she'd trained herself to operate as if she were alone. She'd closed out everything but the task at hand: School, her newspaper work, the business of being mayor. She didn't think about the past or the future, only the present. When she'd returned to Dark River, she'd extended that practice to include extinguishing the memories of Danny Dark.

Insulating herself from memories hadn't been easy, something she'd managed only by avoiding all the places where she'd been with Danny. When that wasn't possible, she'd imposed new activity over the old, and focused on the new. Now he was in her home and his presence was crumbling the walls she'd built.

When she'd agreed to let Danny move in to her guest house so that they could get to know each other again, she hadn't considered that her home would no longer be her sanctuary when he left. And though they'd both like to pretend otherwise, he would leave. She'd spent most of the night resigning herself to that probability. Once she accepted the truth, she could begin to work out their relationship with that knowledge firmly in hand.

They'd loved each other once. Mike was the result of that love. At seventeen their love had been the awkward, wonderful awakening of passion, without distrust or fear. It was only natural that same feeling would spill over into the present. But she needed to know Danny would be there for her and Mike—not off in some foreign country. She wouldn't settle for less.

Katherine hadn't intentionally lived the life of a hermit either before or after she'd returned to Dark River. There'd been several men in her life, including one she'd almost married. And once she'd come home, there had been Joe, who'd always been there for her. But they knew their relationship wasn't destined to ripen now any more than it had when he'd covered for her and Danny.

Danny. For two days her mind had churned with contradicting thoughts of him. At sixteen her plans for the future had centered on a white wedding gown, a church ceremony, and being together forever. That would never be. She wasn't looking for wedding gowns and tradition anymore. She didn't even care about ceremonies and official commitment. All she cared about was Mike and his future. Danny was simply an issue to be resolved. At least that's what she told herself.

For the time Danny was there, she'd let whatever happened happen openly and freely. Beyond that, the future would take care of itself. She wouldn't turn her back on Danny. For Mike's sake, they would learn to be friends. That's all she'd allow herself to expect.

"Aunt Vic and Mike had a stack of sandwiches a mile high in their basket," Katherine said. "Though I don't know where Mike is going to stow it after that breakfast he told me he put away."

"I know, he and I had a nice talk while I was unpacking." Danny was glad for the protection the cool shadows of the study afforded him. In the hallway Katherine was showered with hot sunlight. She was wearing a red dress with a full skirt and a soft cotton top that clung to her body. He could see a damp spot of perspiration between her breasts, breasts that were filled out now, not small and delicate as they'd been when he'd held them in his hands long ago.

"He told me. He also said he thinks that you 'like' him."

Danny released a long breath and lowered his feet to the floor. If he didn't stop his mind from reverting back to the past, he'd be holding her against him every minute—and that was something he'd promised not to do. Slow and easy, he told himself. He had to start over, rebuild this relationship one step at a time. If it was going to work, he couldn't rush it.

He shoved a marker into the journal he was reading, laid it on the desk, and ambled to his feet. "He's right. And yes, a sandwich would be nice."

"I hope you like peanut butter and jelly. I'm

afraid that Mike and Aunt Vic were only concerned for their own taste buds."

Danny's attention locked on the damp spot between Katherine's breasts again. "I absolutely love peanut butter and jelly." He forced his gaze upward.

"Good." She turned toward the kitchen.

"Katherine."

She stopped and waited for him to join her. Danny felt a surge of response to Katherine's nearness.

"You've filled out, Katherine."

"So have you, Danny."

Danny gulped. "Eh, yes, in some ways more than others." He felt an unexpected flush of color in his cheeks.

"What's the matter?" Katherine laughed lightly. "You can look at me, but I'm not supposed to look back? What's wrong, have you turned shy?"

"I always was shy, insecure, awkward. Didn't you notice?" he asked, feeling the air evaporating from the space where they were.

"No. I never did. I thought you were very sure of yourself."

"I wasn't then, and I'm not now. If I were, I'd try to kiss you."

"Neither am I, sure of myself, I mean," she admitted, "but the difference is, I know what I want."

"Oh? What's that?"

"I want my son. But wanting to kiss you takes a definite second place."

"Don't you think we owe it to Mike to at least

explore all the possibilities of our feelings? I really think that a kiss is in both our best interests."

His intention to wait until she had time to think about his question died in his mind as he took an involuntary step toward her.

Caught by the thought of Danny being a shy, insecure little boy, Katherine responded as she always had; she would make things right. Placing her hands on either side of his face, she drew his lips to hers.

"I hope you're right, Danny," she whispered.

"Of course. We need to explore all the possibilities. A kiss might be a reasonable step under the circumstances."

By the time they heard the slamming of the back door, the temperature in the hallway had risen to an alarming degree.

Katherine turned, stepped in front of Danny, and folded her arms across her chest, effectively hiding button-hard nipples jutting against her shirt—and Danny's more obvious sign of desire. Danny let out a breath of relief and annoyance. He followed her closely down the hallway into the kitchen, and dropped gratefully into a chair at the breakfast table.

"Danny, Aunt Vic and I are going to eat our lunch out by the pool. Want to come?" Mike asked.

"Eh, no. I mean not now," Danny managed to reply. "It's too hot out there in the middle of the day."

"It's pretty warm in here, too," Victoria observed with a shrewd look at her niece as Katherine busily filled glasses with ice, reached for the pitcher of tea, realized that they were drinking milk, and started over again. "I didn't know you were coming home to lunch, Katherine."

"Neither did I," Katherine admitted. "I can't stay. I have a meeting with the chamber of commerce about the new plant. Half of them want it and half of them don't."

"And what do you want?" Danny asked curiously.

"What I want isn't important. At the moment it's a moot point anyway. Nobody is willing to put up the capital."

"I don't understand. Why wouldn't the city council support such a project?"

"There are some who feel that it would offer jobs only to outsiders. There aren't many blue-collar workers in Dark River. So it wouldn't mean much to our citizens."

"Only more money in taxes and more money spent in the community," Danny said with a frown.

"Danny's right," Victoria observed as she placed glasses on a tray. "I have an idea. Why don't you take Danny to the meeting with you? Maybe he could talk some sense into those half-wits. Mike and I have plans for this afternoon, and we wouldn't want to disturb anybody."

"Sure," Danny quickly agreed. "But I'd like to have a look at the land-use survey and get a little information together first. Then I'd be glad to offer my advice in locating industry, if you think anybody would be interested."

"I . . . Thank you, Danny. I don't know what the council will say," Katherine began stiffly, then amended her answer, "but I'd appreciate your opinion." Katherine crossed her fingers and hoped she'd be able to get them to listen to Danny. His feedback could be valuable.

Katherine placed the glasses on the table and sat down, feeling a certain amount of satisfaction in knowing that they had another common goal.

"Mike, take our milk outside." Victoria paused in the doorway and asked curiously, "You all right, Katherine? You look a little flushed."

Danny lifted the glass and waited to hear what Katherine would tell her aunt. Their decision to get to know each other for Mike's benefit was one thing, but explaining it to her aunt might be difficult.

"You know that I agreed to let Danny use our library to research his family by reading the original council minutes," Katherine answered.

"I know." Victoria waited.

"Well, there's a bit more to the arrangement than that. Danny and I also have to come to a decision about . . . Mike's future. I told Danny the truth last night."

"I knew you would."

"You did? How?"

"Because you're a woman who understands the need for love. You couldn't deprive Mike of a father, any more than you could turn Danny away."

Katherine didn't realize that Danny had taken her hand until he began squeezing it.

"And what are you planning to do about Mike?" Aunt Vic asked curiously. "It isn't going to take him long to figure out that you two care about each other."

"We don't know," Danny answered when Katherine didn't. "We're going to take it slow; let Mike and I get acquainted, let Katherine and I get to know each other again. We think we owe it to Mike to be friends."

"Uh-huh, and from the look of you I'd say you're moving right along on that part of the agreement. Somehow I get the feeling that Mike and I interrupted something a bit more heavy than friendship?"

The milk Danny was sipping went down the wrong way. Katherine came to her feet and began to pound on his back. Danny swallowed hard. If the milk didn't kill him, Katherine's energetic first-aid would. By the time he regained his composure, Aunt Vic was overcome with laughter.

"Uh-huh. That's what I thought. Well, I consider myself a modern woman, so I'm all for you and Katherine getting to know each other—for Mike's benefit. But you might want to be a bit less obvious around your son."

"Aunt Vic!" Mike called impatiently, "I'm hungry!"

Katherine jerked her hand away from Danny's shoulder.

"Obvious?" Danny repeated. "Are we that obvious?"

Victoria smothered a smile and backed out the door. "Check the thermostat, will you, Katherine? It's much too warm in here. And by the way, Danny, you might want to throw a cloth over that table the next time you decide to hide under it."

Danny looked down.

The top of the table was made of clear glass.

They must have eaten the peanut-butter-and-jelly sandwiches, though Katherine didn't remember tasting them.

They must have told Mike and Victoria good-bye, but Danny's memory was as faulty as Katherine's.

At least he'd changed into a pair of slacks and had put on his shoes, which helped Katherine's mental state only slightly. When they reached city hall, she was still having trouble composing herself.

"Are you sure you want to get involved in this kind of small town industry?" she asked uneasily.

"Why not? If this is going to be my town, I'm willing to offer my services."

"I'm not sure how the committee will react."

"To me, or to us?"

"To, oh, I don't know, Danny. Right now I'm not thinking too clearly. You have a way of doing that to me. And for the next few hours I'm the mayor. I can't allow my feelings for you to show. It would cloud my credibility before the council and might kill the project before it gets started."

"That obvious, are we?"

"I think so. Would you mind waiting until I prepare the council members for your input?"

"Not at all. I'll examine the county engineer's surveys of the site in the meantime. You can tell the committee that I'm going to look over the presentation and give my expert opinion on possible financing." Danny leaned across the seat, lightly brushed Katherine's cheek with his lips, and opened the car door. "Don't worry, Katherine. We'll work it out. I'll be around when you're done."

She watched as he ambled down the sidewalk. He stopped to speak to Fred, Dark River's only barber, the one man who could and would spread the news of that kiss from one end of town to the other.

So much for second thoughts. Their relationship would be public knowledge before Katherine knew what it was. She got out of her car and strode inside city hall, leaving Fred smiling broadly on the street outside.

By the time she had stopped to speak to several businessmen who were to attend the meeting and then had made her way into her office, her secretary, Nancy, was regarding her with much the same smile that Fred had.

"So, he's the one."

"What do you mean, Nancy?"

"The guy you've been waiting for all this time."

"Who said I've been waiting for anybody?"

"Outside of a few casual dates with Joe, you haven't gone out seriously with a man since you got back here five years ago, Katherine Sinclair. I know when a woman has put her life on hold. First you bring home a child, then comes Mr. Tall, Dark, and Intense."

"So you've heard about Danny staying in my guest house. Well, that was Aunt Vic's doing. So don't go making more of it than there is."

The phone began to ring. Katherine swung around and fled into her private office.

"It's Joe Hall, Katherine," Nancy called out.

Katherine picked up the receiver gratefully, "Hello, Joe, what's happening?"

"That's what I'd like to know. What about you and Dan? I thought once was enough."

"So, you heard about the kiss, too?"

"Kiss? No, I called about his moving into the guest house. Are you sure that's a good idea?"

"I'm certain it isn't, Joe. But there's a complication, a reason I hadn't counted on."

"Yeah, and I know the reason. You're still in love with the guy, aren't you?"

"I don't know, Joe. I really don't know. And I'm not even sure it matters now."

"It matters, Katherine. I don't want to see you hurt again. I care."

"Thank you, Joe. You've always been a good friend. But this is something that I have to do."

"I was afraid you'd say that. But I'm here if you need me."

The rest of Katherine's afternoon was devoted to talking with the committee on industrial development. After the meeting Katherine could hear the phone ringing insistently. She was indebted to the girl who was not only her secretary but her friend. She didn't know what Nancy had told the callers, but after a heated debate with herself over what she was going to do about Danny, Katherine finally gathered up her handbag and a briefcase filled with all of the building information to be considered, and left.

She was ready to fall apart.

She hoped that Danny was ready to catch her, even if the world was watching.

Four

When Danny opened the door and slid inside the car, Katherine didn't even look at him.

"That bad, huh?"

"What?"

"Is it the plant or our being together that's turned you into a zombie?"

"Neither—both, I guess. Am I that obvious?"

Danny heard the strain in her voice and searched for a way to make it easier for her. "What did your committee on industry say?"

Katherine jerked her head up guiltily. "They . . . they weren't as enthusiastic as I'd expected them to be."

"You mean that to them I'm still Danny Dark, bad boy."

"No, that's not true, Danny. They know that you're very successful. They know about your company and how you work. They're just bull-headed about listening to an—outsider."

"But I'm not an outsider, Katherine."

This time Katherine heard the quiet pain in his

voice. Heads of corporations, even countries, were willing to pay for Danny's advice, but those in his own hometown were suspicious of his motives. Well, they weren't going to close him out as long as she was mayor. Not if she could help it. He was her son's father.

Katherine drove quickly down one of the side streets and turned away from town. Before she was aware of the direction she was heading, she'd reached the river just beyond the Sinclair estate. Their river, their secret spot.

"Dark River needs your expertise, Danny, and I do not intend to allow a few narrow-minded Neanderthals to tell me what to do. I think we need to talk about this."

"I think we need to talk about us. I don't care about those fools back there. We're what's important."

"But, Danny . . ."

"No, Katherine. This is you-and-me time. Let's find a cool place in the shade and talk."

They got out of the car, deliberately turning away from the place where'd they met as teenagers, each recognizing the need to prevent themselves from being overcome with memories of the past. Danny led her to a swing, placed by the river by some long-ago resident of a tumbled-down house in the distance.

Katherine sat down gingerly, listening to the groan of the chain. "Do you think it's safe?"

"Probably not, but why should this be any different from anything else we've done since I got back to town?"

She felt the swing give from his weight as he sat down beside her. Only the squeak of the chain broke the silence as they began to move slowly back and forth. Beside the grassy bank the black-green water moved silently along. Now and then a splash broke the silence when a fish jumped in the distance. Dragonflies floated gracefully along the water's edge, and the occasional croak of a frog added to the familiarity of the setting.

"I've missed this river," Danny admitted. "I didn't know how much. Why did you come back, Katherine? You'd made a life away from Dark River."

"Because Aunt Vic is getting old. She worried about me. This is my home, and I felt as though I needed to come back and face it. Does that make any sense?"

"I think so. The past, the present, the future, they all get jumbled together. One doesn't exist except in relationship to the other. That's why I'm going to find out about my family. Not just for Mike, but for myself, too. Then I may just rub the noses of the fine residents of Dark River in the truth before I leave."

"There it is again—the word *leave*." Katherine wrapped her arms around her middle and tried to quell the shaking that had already started.

Danny slid his arm across the edge of the swing, feeling Katherine tense up as he touched her back. The moisture on her neck beneath her hair was hot against his skin. The ends of her hair tickled his bare arm and sent a shiver through his body.

He took a deep breath and reluctantly moved his arm away. This was a time for talking, not touching. Touching would come, he was certain, but not yet.

"We have to talk about that, Katherine. You know I want to be Mike's father," Danny began. "But if you think it would be better for me to leave for good, I will. I just don't want to screw things up again. Can you believe that?"

"Yes. I went through the same thing myself after the attorney called. I had to ask myself whether bringing Mike to Dark River was in his best interest. I couldn't tell Mike that he was my child, and I was afraid that somebody would find out and tell him before I was ready. I didn't know if it would be fair to Mike. Before I could get all that worked out, you arrived."

"So, what are you going to do about me?"

"That appears to be a rhetorical question, since we already know you're—temporary."

"Maybe, maybe not. I have to come back somewhere, sometime."

"Sure, Danny, just drop by when it's convenient. I don't know whether I can handle that." She gathered up her courage and continued as honestly as she could. "We've already agreed that the attraction between us is still there. What I don't know is if there's anything else."

Katherine was avoiding looking at him. The familiar telltale blush of uncertainty had colored her cheeks, bringing his every primitive feeling close to the surface. "Suppose," he ventured, "suppose you decide there isn't any us? What does that do to Mike?"

"I don't know. I don't think it's going to be as simple as either one of us thought, is it?"

This time she did turn and look at him. Danny thought he'd never seen anything as beautiful as the woman beside him. Her eyes were moist and wide; her proud, full mouth drawn tightly in a challenge.

The sound of a distant airplane moving across the sky was drowned out by the beating of his heart.

Oh, yes, Danny's girl had changed, she'd grown stronger. There was an emotional strength and courage about her that had been missing ten years before. Where she'd once been pliable beneath his touch, she was now in control—fragile, but in control.

Danny reached out, took her hand, and slowly turned it palm up. Lowering his lips, he kissed the center, brushing her skin softly. Then he threaded his fingers between hers and dropped their clasped hands to his thigh as he took a deep breath and leaned back. This touching was a simple gesture of promise, his promise that they were together again.

"You're right, darling," he said, "it isn't simple. But then nothing worth having ever is. And you and Mike are the most important part of my life now."

"Yes," she whispered, "for now," and lifted her foot from the ground, allowing the swing to move back and forth again. A butterfly drifted into view. Beyond the trees in the distance the blue sky seemed brighter than it had a moment before.

"Did you know that this place was originally the site of a Creek Indian village?" Katherine was lying sprawled on the floor of the study, as she read the journal open before her.

"No, I didn't know." In fact Danny was having a hard time concentrating on anything beyond her long, slim legs and her rounded bottom enclosed in a pair of tight shorts.

"Yep, we took it away from them with a treaty that promised we'd never ask for more."

"That doesn't surprise me," Danny said with an odd strain in his voice. "The good people of Dark River have always had a way of doing what they wanted and making it sound as if they were acting under some kind of special authorization."

"Just imagine," Katherine mused, "these ledgers have been stored here all my life and I never opened one of them. I'm the mayor. I can't believe that I've been so disinterested in my own town."

"Well, you've had other things on your mind."

"I certainly have for the last few days," she agreed dreamily, closing the ledger. She slid it away from her, stretching her arms straight out as she lay down flat on the floor. "Trampolines, hiking. You and your son can really wear a person out. I could honestly lie here on the floor and go to sleep. I don't know when I've been so lazy on a Saturday."

"But it's been good, hasn't it? The three of us together?"

"Yes, it has." She yawned and turned over on her back.

"You're very good with Mike, you know. He likes you."

Katherine smiled. "I like him, too, when he isn't putting worms in my shoes or screaming over some game with Aunt Vic."

Danny laughed. "You're right. When they're together, it's hard to tell which one is the kid."

Katherine yawned again. "Where is our son, anyway. After what he's put me through for the last week, he's awfully quiet this afternoon."

Our son. The very sound of those words took his breath away. Spending the afternoon in the study with Katherine had been nice. Wondering casually about their son made the picture complete.

If the sight of Katherine's backside had been a distraction to Danny, the front side totally wiped him out. He closed his eyes and groaned. Having Katherine help him with his research might not turn out to be a rational move as far as his original quest was concerned, but it was definitely strong motivation for hastening the development of the relationship.

"Our son and Aunt Vic were heading for the train garden, I think he called it. What in the world is that? I can vouch from experience that this place grows some pretty spectacular products, but trains?"

"You've never seen the train garden?" Katherine came to her feet and held out her hand. "That's right, Aunt Vic hadn't refurbished it when you used to sneak onto the grounds and throw rocks at my window at night. Come, I'll show you."

All things considered, seeing a train garden was a more reasonable activity than the one his mind kept settling on. This time he didn't have a glass table to hide beneath. This time it took a long walk across a lawn filled with two-hundred-year-old oaks to accomplish the same purpose.

The secluded garden, enclosed by the three-foot-high rock wall, appeared empty. In one corner a small fish pond nestled into the curve of the wall. Lined with moss-covered rocks, the wall rose on a gradual incline to form the enclosure for the water. Across in the other corner was what appeared to be a volcano.

"What do you think?"

Danny's answer was delayed by the sound of a train whistle, a low, lonely whistle that seemed muffled until Danny realized it was coming from inside the volcano. As he watched, a rather large toy train exited and sped out onto a track that ran along the edge of the rock wall.

A smile broke across Danny's face. "A train! I don't believe it, a real toy train." He followed its progress along the wall, past a bank of marigolds, and around the curve that began to drop down onto what he now recognized as a trestle over the fish pond.

The cars rolled and shimmied. The engine belched little puffs of smoke, and the whistle gave another series of long, lonely wails, just as it went under a bush and disappeared from sight.

The sound of Mike's laughter pulled Danny's attention to the brick wall behind the shrubs where the train had vanished.

"I take it that Aunt Vic is into trains as well as video games?"

"You got it. Come inside and see her real love."

Climbing a set of stone steps that formed a second tunnel for the tracks running around the garden wall, Katherine led Danny inside a small building into another world; a miniature world of trains and villages and a full circus ground. In the midst of the make-believe world were Aunt Vic and Mike. Both wore blue engineers' caps and red bandannas around their necks.

"Look, Danny, isn't this neat? A house full of trains that don't go anywhere. They run around the house, out into the garden, and come right back here."

Katherine smiled. Mike liked the trains because he could control where they went. He liked them staying in one place. That brought a tear to her eye. She knew exactly what he meant.

"Aunt Vic is the engineer, Danny, and I'm the assistant. Want to blow the whistle?"

Danny was speechless. "How in the world did you do all this, Aunt Vic?"

"Oh, I didn't. I mean I only cleaned it up and got it going again. It was started by Katherine's great-great-uncle back in the twenties. He collected the steam-operated trains, and every Sinclair since, up until Katherine's father, added to the line. Welcome to Dark River Railroad Junction."

"What happened to old Samuel? Trains didn't interest him?"

"No. That was one part of the Sinclair heritage he couldn't identify with. Trains were playthings, and he never took time to play. Here, Danny. You have a go at being the engineer." Aunt Vic stepped away from her position at the roundhouse control panel.

But Danny made no attempt to take Victoria's place. Instead he stood awkwardly, frowning.

Katherine watched his puzzling reaction, then realized where the problem lay. Danny had never learned how to play. He was embarrassed in front of Mike.

"You two run the train," Katherine said quickly, "Danny and I will start up the circus. Come and give me a hand, Mr. Dark."

Within minutes Katherine had brought the amusement park to life. Little lights along the outer edge of the Ferris wheel began to blink, and the wheel started to turn. The swings, occupied by tiny plastic people, splayed out in a circle around the pole at the center. And the carousel started up, its small animals jerking around in a ripple of up-and-down motion. The blinking and turning were accompanied by the sound of a calliope.

Switches clicked, rerouting trains to side tracks, holding them in a waiting pattern, before sending them on their way again. Large passenger cars with tiny figures at the windows made their way merrily along, while smaller working engines directed cars filled with logs and cattle into side yards for unloading. Danny watched the procedure in complete awe.

Though Danny had accumulated vast wealth, property, and a certain amount of prestige, Katherine knew he'd never learned the simple pleasures of just playing. He'd never owned a train. He'd never had toys. Until he'd "found" one while in third grade, he'd never ridden a bicycle.

That incident had been his first real scrape with the law. It had been Katherine who'd rescued him. She'd explained to the teacher that she'd found the bike near the playground, and because it was a boy's bike, she'd asked Danny to ride it to school.

The bicycle had started it all, started Katherine's defense of Danny Dark. He'd been a wise kid from the only street in Dark River that wasn't listed on the city map. And his defender had been the princess on the hill, a princess whose ancestors had a garden just for trains. Now she was defending him again, against the stupidity of a city council who would give up a plant that would provide jobs for citizens badly in need of employment rather than run the risk of bringing more blue-collar workers into the town. Katherine had concealed their true concerns from Danny, but he'd managed to poke around and find out.

In the years he'd been away, he'd changed his life. There was a new tolerance about him. He was determined to find a way to win over the members of the city council and make himself a part of Dark River no matter what it took—for Mike.

Katherine and Aunt Vic left Danny and Mike with the trains and went to the house to prepare supper. By the time it was ready, Danny had mastered every control in the train house.

After supper Danny and Katherine sat on the porch and watched the fireflies frantically signaling their telegraphic love calls in the black night. Aunt Vic had gone to bed, and Mike was watching television.

"You loved growing up here, didn't you, Katherine?"

"After Aunt Vic came, yes. Though for a long time she wasn't a real part of the family the way she is now. The guest house was always hers, but my father didn't like too much interference from her inside the house. He kept very strict boundaries, and we knew what they were."

"I don't understand. Your mother was dead, you were only a child. Why wouldn't he welcome his own sister to help raise you?"

"Aunt Vic wasn't my father's sister. Willingham was my mother's maiden name. Aunt Vic was my mother's sister. And Father was always afraid that people would talk. He wouldn't tolerate any threat of gossip. You ought to know that."

"Your father was a hard man. Didn't he like your aunt? I guess that was a stupid question. I don't think Samuel Sinclair ever really liked anybody."

"When I was a child, I never thought he liked her much. But now, when I look back, I wonder."

Danny turned his head. His eyes had adjusted to the darkness, and he could see the silvery strands of Katherine's hair like a feathery cloud of moonlight around her face. He felt contented here with her, with Mike, with Aunt Vic. He was tired after hours of nothing but play. He'd never spent such a day in his life. And he'd never been happier.

"You wonder about what?" he asked, rocking slowly back and forth.

"They were always a bit strained around each other, Daddy and Aunt Vic, as if they didn't quite know how to act. Daddy was a lot older than my mother, you know. She was twenty, and he was forty when they were married. She was thirty-five when I was born. I was a disappointment to him. He'd wanted a boy."

"He'd have liked Mike. Too bad he didn't . . ." Danny let his voice trail off. The subject would only make Katherine uncomfortable. But, dammit, in spite of what Samuel Sinclair had done to him, he couldn't believe that the man never cared enough about his daughter to show her a little affection. No wonder Katherine had no faith in men. The only two she'd ever cared about had failed her. Old Sam hadn't wanted her, and he himself had deserted her.

"Too bad he didn't know his grandson?" Katherine finished Danny's sentence. "You can't know how many times I've wished for that. But . . . tell me about you, Danny. Where have you been since you left Dark River and how did you get so rich?"

Danny laughed. "The truth or the official biography?"

"The truth, if there is such a thing."

"It all started in college. I had a professor who was a tinkerer. He had the ideas, but he didn't know what to do with them. The inventing was all he cared about, not the application of his product. Let's just say that we worked out an exchange of services."

"Let's see if I can interpret an 'exchange of services,'" Katherine said, allowing a smile to play across her lips. "I'd say that you wanted something he had. In return you gave him something he needed. Is that about it?"

"Yep, I needed an *A* in his class, and he needed a backer for his water purification system."

"And you found one?"

"I did."

"And you got an *A*?"

"Nope, the old piker flunked me. But I got a piece of the water system, and the company that bought it thought that was a fair exchange."

"Cupcakes." Katherine said with a sigh.

"Cupcakes? I don't understand."

"I remember the first time I ever saw you, Danny. You were promising one of the kids in our first grade class that you'd protect us from the mob in exchange for his cupcake."

"Oh, yeah. As I recall he thought it was a good exchange."

"As I recall, there were no mobs in the first grade."

"You see, it worked."

"Ah, Danny, you'll never change. What happened then? Did you graduate?"

"Yep, believe it or not, I graduated from UCLA with a degree in engineering and special training in marketing."

"UCLA? No wonder I couldn't find you. When you left town, you went a long way. I'm sorry about your dad, Danny. Aunt Vic wrote to me when he died. It was a tragic accident."

Danny let a long time pass before he spoke. "It was no accident, Katherine. He took off all his clothes and walked into Dark River. Appropriate, huh? He was killed by the river he always claimed had been named for his family."

"The river is deceiving, isn't it? Parts of it are treacherous, particularly when the dam upriver is opened to release the overflow. That's one of the things I've tried to do as mayor, to see that the dangerous places are well marked and an alarm is sounded before the dam water is released. We've cut down the accident rate considerably."

"Katherine, you don't understand. It wasn't an accident. My father never learned to swim. As much as he loved the river, he also feared it."

"Oh, no. I'm so sorry. I keep saying that, don't I? It must have been very hard for you, losing him like that."

"I'd lost him long ago. He just made the loss final. After that I never came back. I thought I didn't fit in here. I'm still not sure that I do."

I came back, Katherine wanted to say, *and it wasn't easy for me either.* She'd made a life for herself—without Danny. She wouldn't have welcomed him then. Her own hurt had been too strong.

"I have something to ask you," Katherine finally said, trying not to hear the uneven crack in her voice. "Aunt Vic, Mike, and I go to church every Sunday. We'd like you to come with us in the morning."

Danny brought his rocker to a stop. "Why would you want me to do that?"

"Because I think our son ought to live a normal life, and if you're trying to see us as a family unit, you need to go all the way while you're here. After all, in spite of what we've said, this is an experiment, isn't is? And sometimes experiments fail."

"I suppose," he admitted reluctantly. "But if it is, you'll be the one to call it off. All I need to know is whether or not I fit into your life."

"And suppose you decide that you don't? I won't let Mike be hurt, Danny."

Katherine left her chair and walked over to the kitchen door. She pushed it open, stopped, and turned back to Danny. "You know that I still care for you, Danny." She started into the house.

"Wait, don't go in yet." Danny sprang to his feet and walked over to the doorway where Katherine was standing. "I want—"

"What do you want, Danny?"

"I don't know. Yes, I do." He caught a strand of silver hair and brushed it back from her forehead. "I want to touch your hair. I want to feel you against me. I want to . . ." He groaned. "Ah, Katherine, I don't know if I can keep away from you."

"I know," she murmured, and leaned against

the wall by the door. She swallowed hard and tried not to tremble. Danny had questioned her keeping her identity a secret from Mike, and she'd tried to give him a truthful answer. She just hadn't told him all of it. Yes, she wanted her son. There'd never been a question of that. But more and more she couldn't escape the knowledge that she wanted Danny, too. Ten years of recrimination had taught her that. She'd been alone long enough to understand how much she wanted him.

She felt his warm breath on her hair. A muted word slipped out as his hands slid around her waist and pulled her against him.

"Ah, Katherine."

This time when he kissed her it wasn't rough, it wasn't quick, and it definitely wasn't a simple good night. He caught her, lifting her into him so that every part of him was caressing every part of her. His touch was as hot as boiling water—the kind of heat that came from 110 degrees and no shade. Perspiration dripped down between her breasts, and a rush of hot moisture pooled between her legs.

Unlocking his hands from behind her back, he moved around her, seeking and finding those parts of her body that ached for his touch. Fingertips slid inside her blouse, setting off a wave of sensation that spiraled downward at the same moment the other hand moved under the waistband of her shorts.

The erratic pounding of her heart increased, nudging a familiar moment from her past into her consciousness—she and Danny, loving each other again.

"Danny," she murmured, pressing herself against him.

"Ah, Katherine, I need you so." He groaned, and slowly, reluctantly pulled back. They were both breathing hard. Her blouse was unbuttoned, and he was holding her bare breast in his hand, rubbing her nipple with his thumb.

"I need you, too, Danny."

He took another deep breath, paused, and let it out again. "Don't whisper like that, Katherine. That's the way you always whispered when we made love, all deep and throaty. I may have more control than I had when I was seventeen, but unless you're better prepared than I, my darling, being caught by your Aunt Vic isn't the greatest risk we'd take."

"Oh!" Katherine pushed against his chest. Madness had swept her away, caught her up in a past that seemed more real than the present. "No! Not again," she cried. She whirled around and ducked into the kitchen before Danny could stop her. What had she expected? She'd practically asked him to make love to her right there on the porch. She'd kissed him. She'd touched him.

She'd wanted him just as much now as she had when she was seventeen. Only now she knew the danger of falling in love with a man who'd left her once and had already told her he would do it again. Her mind and her body screamed at the unfairness with every step she climbed.

Of course she wasn't prepared. There wasn't

another man in her life now. And Danny hadn't come prepared either. He hadn't planned to make love to her. He said he still cared for her. But he'd been in love with her ten years ago, and he'd allowed himself to be bought off by something more important to him, something she couldn't compete with—success.

Katherine hadn't realized she was sobbing until she heard Aunt Vic's anxious voice. "Are you all right, Katherine?"

"No! I mean, yes. I mean, I don't know. Go back to bed, Aunt Vic. I have to figure this out for myself."

"All right, Katherine, but be careful. No, that's not what I want to say. Don't be careful. If you want Danny Dark, go after him. Don't assume that you're wrong for each other, and don't be noble. Hiding your feelings and living a lie could cost you everything you care about."

Katherine stopped. Something about her aunt's words were different. She wasn't sure she understood, but she got the distinct impression that Victoria Willingham wasn't talking about her niece, but about herself.

She took that thought to bed with her, but she couldn't sleep. Finally, as she had done so many nights in the past, she pulled on her robe and opened the cedar chest at the foot of her bed.

Buried beneath an extra blanket and her old cheerleading costumes was the object of her search—a small brown furry bear. She'd bought it for the baby she'd never see, something from his real mother. But they hadn't even given it to him. Later it had become her only comfort. Night after night she'd cried on it, snuggled it, and slept with it in her empty arms.

Carrying it with her now, she slipped across the hall and stood in the darkness by her son's bed. It was time that she told him the truth. She had to find a way.

At daylight, no nearer to finding a solution than before, Katherine got up, pulled on a red swimsuit, and went to the pool. The temperature was already climbing when she dove into the cool water. By the time she'd made her laps, the sky was light and the world had come alive.

Birds chattered noisily. Somewhere in the distance a lawn mower was cranked up. City hall would likely get a call the next morning about somebody breaking the ordinance against the operation of equipment before noon on Sunday.

From his window across the garden, Danny watched as Katherine swam. She was wearing a suit that fit like a second skin. He wanted to be there with her, not just this day but the next, and next month, next year.

Church on Sunday morning. A normal, real family activity. Dare he believe that such a future was possible? He was here now, but in spite of his success, he wasn't certain that Danny Dark could ever truly come back to Dark River and stay. Once he'd thought differently. He'd reached for the brass ring, and he'd been slapped in the face. Outside of Dark River he might be successful. Here he was still that bad boy, Danny Dark. He knew it. Inside of him, that knowledge festered. And Katherine's wanting it to be different wouldn't make it so.

Mike had to be the important issue. Everything bad in his life was here in Dark River. Except now everything good was here too.

Katherine finally left the pool and walked slowly into the house. Danny turned back to his closet and began to flip through his clothes.

What did people in Dark River wear to church on Sunday? He didn't know. He'd never been to church before.

Five

"Is everybody in town a member of this church?"

Danny was having second thoughts about his decision to accompany Katherine and Aunt Vic to Sunday services.

"Can't we just slip in and sit in the back?"

"Not a chance, Danny," Aunt Vic answered. "Every pew in the front of the church has the name of the founding family that paid for it. The Sinclair pew is where we'll be expected to sit."

"I thought you said this would be simple," Danny said between clenched teeth.

"I lied," Katherine said without moving her lips.

Every eye was turned on them as they walked down the aisle.

In spite of his reservations Danny watched with pride as a freshly scrubbed Mike reached out for a hymn book and held it open for Aunt Vic. Danny smiled and followed suit, opening the songbook for him and Katherine. He might not know about church procedure, but he knew hymns, especially the old ones. That was the one legacy his father had passed on. Whenever he'd had a little corn liquor in him, Will Dark had started singing. If Will sang, Danny had to sing with him.

When Katherine heard Danny's deep baritone voice join in, a warm, exquisite feeling of pride swept over her. Here she was, in her town, in her church, on Sunday morning with her family. The world didn't know, but she did. The feeling might not last, but for now, this morning, this hour, this family was hers, and she felt her heart swell.

After the services they were forced to stop and speak to everybody in town. Other than a few scowls in Danny's direction, and a few curious looks from Mike to Katherine and back again, they were caught up in a sea of smiling faces and invitations to "come for dinner," or "Do join us at the club for a game of racquetball," or "Katherine, why didn't you tell us that Danny was back in town?" or "What a fine young boy Mike is. We need him in our Boy Scout troop."

"Katherine, get me out of here," Danny pleaded. "I feel like one of those lab insects pinned on a specimen board."

"Sorry." She laughed lightly and turned away, conscious of his strong hand against the small of her back. The gesture was one of possession. "You're the biggest attraction in town."

"Attraction I approve of," he leaned down and whispered in her ear as he opened her car door and assisted her inside, "so long as it's the private, physical kind."

* * *

Lunch was fried chicken, fresh creamed corn, tomatoes, and corn bread, and it lasted much, much too long. By the time Aunt Vic asked for orders for apple pie, Danny practically growled his refusal. "No thanks, Katherine and I are going for a drive."

"Oh, great. Can I go, Danny?" Mike was eager to come along, until he heard Aunt Vic clear her throat. At the sound he wiped the excitement from his face and glanced at the elderly woman with a sheepish expression on his face. "Oh, yes. I forgot. Aunt Vic and I have . . . a previous commitment."

"That's good," Danny said, "because your—Katherine and I have an appointment, too." He stood up impatiently.

Katherine had a hard time concealing her astonishment. "We do? Where?"

"We're going to . . . to . . ."

"Check out that map I found in Samuel's papers?" Aunt Vic innocently finished his sentence for him.

"Yes, the map," Danny agreed. "I forgot to tell you, Katherine. Aunt Vic gave me an original map of the area this morning while you were getting ready for church. It details a grant of a tract of land to a family named Dark."

"Really?" Katherine's interest wasn't feigned. She quickly began stacking the dishes to clear the table. A section of land that might have belonged to Danny's family was what he'd been looking for, maybe it was enough to keep him in Dark River, at least periodically.

Victoria stepped in front of Katherine and claimed the plates. "That's all right, Katherine, we'll take care of the dishes today. You two change your clothes and get out of here. Mike and I have some serious plotting to do."

Aunt Vic's words registered when Katherine was halfway to the door. She stopped and turned back. "I don't think I like the sound of that. What kind of plotting do you mean?"

"Oh, nothing drastic. Don't worry. We don't have to bring our project up at the town hall meeting for approval. We're just trying to decide what kind of addition Mike would make to Dark River Railroad Junction—*if* he were a member of the Sinclair family. After all, every generation makes its mark. And Samuel didn't contribute a thing."

"Oh." Katherine turned and went up the steps. The addition of a train car or another piece of equipment didn't sound too bad. She was safe giving her silent approval to a project like that. What she wasn't sure about was giving her approval to a drive with Danny Dark. He was dangerous, even in the daytime.

"This can't be right." Katherine flipped her red-framed eyeglasses from the top of her head to her nose and studied the map intently.

Dan opened the car door and got out. "Why not? The map has the official state seal. It very plainly says the land beginning at the big rock by the shoals and proceeding west to what was called, even then, Hangman's Hill, and then southwest to the river again, belonged to the Darks."

Katherine dropped the map and looked up at Danny in consternation. "So, even if this land were part of an original land grant to one Daniel David Dark in 1790, that doesn't mean anything. All this land belonged to somebody once. It was divided, sold, and resold hundreds of times."

"Not this land, at least not all of it," Dan said firmly. "My dear old dad always swore that his father told him the land still belonged to the Darks."

Katherine walked to the water's edge and dropped down to the mossy bank. "It's just that I wouldn't want you to be disappointed, Danny, if it turns out to be a fantasy."

"Oh, I don't know." He sauntered over and stood looking down at her, eyes glazed in passion. "If the fantasy is anything like what I'm seeing right now, I'd die happy."

She looked up, taking in the sight of him towering above her. He was still the most exciting man she'd ever seen—lithe, sizzling with raw passion, his lips clenched in some desperate attempt to restrain himself. "I just want you to be prepared for whatever happens," she said.

"This time I am, Katherine. Whenever you're ready—if you're ready—I'm prepared."

"Oh!" She came to her feet in surprise. She hadn't been thinking of making love, had she? Yes, she had. Why lie to herself? She'd thought of little else ever since they'd driven away from the house. Every time they were together, the need grew.

Standing was a mistake. She was closer to him. As he slowly bent his head, Katherine felt herself sway toward him. "Danny, we can't, not here on the riverbank on a Sunday afternoon. Half the city is likely to come rafting by at any moment."

"So, we'll go somewhere else, somewhere private."

He still wasn't touching her. Katherine shuddered with anticipation. He didn't need to touch her. She was on fire simply being close to him.

"I don't know. You tell me. There must be some place we can be together, completely together. I want to hold you in my arms, feel your bare body sliding like silk against mine."

"Oh, Danny, I'm afraid. It's happening all over again, isn't it? That's what you used to say to me every time we met at this river."

"And you told me every time that there was no place we could go without being recognized, even if we'd had the money for a motel room."

"Well, that hasn't changed." She laughed lightly.

"Would you care if somebody recognized us checking into the River Inn?"

Katherine stepped back and lowered her gaze uneasily. "I think I would," she admitted. "Not so much that I'd care, but I'd feel uncomfortable. The good feelings are still there, Danny, but the others are there, too. I don't want to fall in love with you all over again, knowing that you're going to leave."

Suddenly the mood of the day changed, and Dan didn't know how to bring the lightness back. Being with Katherine wasn't a problem for him, but Katherine was afraid to care for him. It wasn't her father's shadow that fell over them now, it was distrust. He knew that Katherine wanted him. He was reasonably certain that the want went deeper than just desire. If he could only get her away from Dark River, he was sure she'd come to him willingly. But if she gave him her trust, could he go when the time came? He didn't know.

Dan reached out and laid his hand on Katherine's shoulder. "It's all right, darling. We'll work it out. We have to. We're a team, you and me. Us against the Dark River City Council, remember?"

Slowly she began to relax as the tension drained away from her body. This was Danny, her Danny, and she wanted him more than anything in the world. It was just that every time she felt him reaching for her, she began to draw back. Her body seemed to go into some weird kind of automatic shutdown just before it reached the point of no return.

"I'm sorry," she said with a sad smile. "I really don't care what anybody thinks. It's just that I . . . I mean I can't seem to believe very much in forever. It was different before. We were in love."

Irritated, Dan turned his face away. "And you think we aren't now?"

"I . . . I don't know what I think. I just know that you're going away." Her voice sounded so desolate.

Dan turned back to look at her. He squeezed her shoulder and gave her a kiss on her forehead. "Maybe forever isn't here yet."

"Maybe it isn't going to be, either."

"As Aunt Vic used to say, let's not get carried away with what might have been and lose sight of what's happening now. And right now we have land surveying to do. I didn't want to say anything because without the map I couldn't prove it, but I located the minutes of the council that drew up the original boundaries for the city.

"The minutes say that each landholder agreed to donate a portion of land to be used for the common good for two hundred years, afterward the land could be bought from the original landholder for fair market value. In the event the land was of no further use then, or later, it would revert back to the original family or its heirs. In this case the Dark family. That's me. Other than Mike there are no more Darks."

Katherine pushed off the last of her reservations and joined in the search. "And how can you be sure about that? You didn't know about Mike."

Dan winced. "I know, but I promise you, Katherine, there was never an opportunity for another Mike. You're the only woman I ever lost my head over. As for other heirs . . ." He laughed confidently. "I had a lady-friend a few years ago who was into genealogy. She researched my family, just to see if I was proper husband material."

"Aha! And were you?"

"She thought so. I didn't."

"Old love-'em-and-leave-'em Dark," she said without thinking. Seeing the look of pain rack his face, she suddenly realized what she'd alluded to. "Danny, I didn't mean that the way it sounded."

"Perhaps not, but it's true, isn't it? It's there in the back of your mind all the time, isn't it, Katherine? You want to be with me, but you don't trust me. You expect me to hurt you again. What if it isn't like that this time?"

Katherine laid two fingers across his lips, silencing his accusation with her silent plea. "What if it is, Danny? I don't think anything. I'm not going to think anything. I never expected to see my son again. Nothing you could do would ever diminish what I feel about having him back. Trust is a word I don't know much about. Trust is something I'm trying very hard to learn."

Dan caught her fingers and pulled them away. He drew her close and frowned. "Katherine, I . . . dammit, I'm sorry. I keep pinning you down, backing you into a corner. It's just that you're so beautiful. Standing there like an angel. The sky matches your eyes. It's so blue it feels as if we're standing in the sky."

"One more step," she said wryly, "and we'll be standing in water."

Danny glanced at their feet. He'd been more right than he knew about backing her into a corner, except this time the corner was the riverbank.

"I could kiss you, Katherine. There's no room for you to evade me this time. But I won't. I know that this has all come as a shock to you. Maybe I'm bathing in memories of what we once had, too. But I don't think so. Ever since I saw you in your office that morning, it's been like a dream."

"That's what I'm afraid of, afraid that it's all a lovely dream. But dreams turn into nightmares."

"Not that kind of dream, Katherine. Haven't you ever dreamed something and known that you'd dreamed it before? You're struggling, uncertain, and then you go into a room or a place and a sigh of relief comes over you as you recognize it, and you know that you'll be all right. That's the way I feel now."

This time when he lowered his head, Katherine didn't struggle. When he settled his mouth against hers, she pressed herself against him, feeling the strength of him, feeling the primitive need that was always there, just below the surface. As she gave herself to the kiss she tried for one moment to think. There must be a place for them. They had to be together, if not forever, then once more in a dream. Maybe there was no happily ever after. Maybe there was only now.

By the time Danny lifted her in his arms and turned away from the river, Katherine was past saying no.

"Where? Where are we going?" she asked dreamily.

"We're going to the car, my darling, before I forget that we're on a public shore on a Sunday afternoon in June."

"Oh!" Katherine said, realizing that the distant echo she'd been hearing in her mind wasn't part of her dream but the intrusion of reality. A series of inner tubes, tied together like a rack of billiard balls, was floating lazily downstream.

"You'd better put me down, Danny, before we're discovered."

"If you're sure that's what you want." He opened the door to the convertible and started to lower her to the seat.

"Wait, the map." Katherine reached behind her and found the paper. She waited for Danny to release her. "Well, are you going to let me go?"

"Do I have to? Couldn't we just pretend that you've sprained your ankle, that the car has broken down?"

"How far do you think we'd get?"

"Just out of sight of the river?" He lifted his lips into a wicked smile and slid Katherine up and down against his chest.

"That's what I'm afraid of," Katherine said, her voice low and husky.

"Are you afraid of me, Katherine?"

"No, I'm afraid of me, afraid that I won't be able to let you go."

"Hello, Mayor Sinclair," a voice called out merrily from the flotilla moving past.

"Good to see you in church, Dan," another joined in.

"Now, see what you've done. Put me down, Danny."

"You're right. The damage is done." Dan kissed Katherine quickly and deposited her beside the car. "So there's no need to retreat."

"Oh, yes, there is," Katherine argued, unrolling the map and laying it out on the hood of the car while she studied it intently. She tried not to hear the cheers from the river, forcing herself instead to concentrate on the faded map with its wavy lines. Suddenly she caught her breath.

"What's wrong?" Dan leaned across the hood beside her.

Katherine's mind was racing. She was no attorney, but if this map was authentic—and she had no reason to believe it wasn't—the town of Dark River could be in big trouble.

"Danny, you say the minutes placed the donated land at a point where they all joined."

"That's what they said."

"And your family offered a portion of their land for the common good?"

"Yes. This map shows the Dark grant. Apparently only a part of each owner's land was actually used. The reference in the minutes is to a section of land surrounding something called Hangman's Hill. The rest of the Dark property was retained by my illustrious family, at least for a while before they lost it."

"I see."

"What's wrong, Katherine? You look as if you've seen a ghost."

"Eh, no." Katherine stood up and leaned against the fender of the car. "What do you intend to do if the minutes are correct?"

"Do? About what?"

"About reclaiming the land. If my arithmetic is right, 1790 to 1990 is two hundred years. The time has come for Hangman's Hill to be returned to you."

Dan laughed and looped his arms around Katherine's waist. "Why, I'll probably check the location out, and then, who knows, maybe I'll build a house there."

"Suppose," she said in a low voice, "suppose the land isn't suitable for a house?"

"Well, I'll put something else there. Wouldn't it give my father a big laugh if a Dark really did contribute something important to Dark River? What would you like me to build in our town, Katherine, an office building? What about a toy manufacturing company? Aunt Vic and Mike could play all the time."

"Danny, I think I ought to tell you that if this map is correct, the land that you own is the section of downtown Dark River on which the city square is built."

"You're kidding?"

"Not only that, but it also includes the land the city council is feuding about. The property, where the lawn furniture company may or may not be built, encompasses the street where you used to live."

"Well, what do you know about that? Looks like the city council is going to have to deal with Dan Dark whether they want to or not."

"Yes." And so is the mayor, she wanted to add as they drove back home.

"Aunt Vic, have you ever heard anything about the history of Hangman's Hill?"

They were having breakfast, Aunt Vic, Mike, Katherine, and Danny.

"I seem to remember that your father mentioned something once. I think it was when they had the dedication ceremony for the statue of General Sinclair in the park."

"General Sinclair," Mike joined in. "He's in the battlefield at the barbershop."

"Oh, yes, the one where the men stage the Revolutionary War all over again. Don't believe them, boy," Aunt Vic cautioned. "They rewrite history regularly."

"Yeah," Mike said, "they said that the first Dark here was a Tory, that he sold out to the English."

"That wasn't unusual." Katherine defended David Dark. "Savannah was settled by the English, and the settlers retained ties with the mother country because their families were still there."

Victoria refilled Mike's glass with milk and plopped a second piece of bread into the toaster. "By the way, Katherine, I hope that you don't have anything planned for Saturday."

"Why? What's going on, Aunt Vic?"

"Mike has been invited to join the local Boy Scout troop. They're having a camp-out at the river. I've arranged for you and Danny to go along as chaperons. I was sure you wouldn't mind."

"You did what?" Katherine couldn't hide the surprise in her voice.

"Chaperons. I figure you two are experienced enough to handle that, don't you?"

Katherine looked at the expression on Mike's

face, at Danny, then back at Aunt Vic. This time her aunt was going too far.

"Sure," Danny agreed, "I think that is a splendid idea. Katherine will love it."

His grin was short-lived when Aunt Vic said, "You won't be the only adults going along."

Katherine narrowed her gaze and pursed her lips. "Say, I thought that Scout camping trips were all-male affairs."

"Not anymore," Aunt Vic said conspiratorially. "These are the liberated nineties. We don't have a Girl Scout troop here in Dark River, so they let three girls join the boys. What do you think, Mike?"

"I don't know, Aunt Vic," Mike said, his face filled with uncertainty. "What if the guys don't like me? I mean I wasn't in school with them long enough to get to know any of them."

"Why of course they'll like you!" Katherine stood up, anger pulsing through her body. She quelled the urge to take the boy in her arms and hold him. What had the students been saying to Mike?

"Did they say anything unkind to you in school, Mike? I realize that we don't have any close neighbors for you to play with, but I thought you were getting along all right."

"They asked about my mom and pop. I . . . I just said they died in a crash. But it's hard sometimes when the other guys talk about . . . well, you know, family things."

Katherine felt as if a sheet of ice had been dropped over her. She felt Mike's frustration. And she felt her own, too. She had decided not to hover over Mike. She had legal custody of him. She'd been afraid to push for more than that. But she could see now that she'd been wrong.

"The Scout trip sounds like fun," Katherine said enthusiastically. "And maybe afterward, we'll ask some of the guys over to swim, and play with your trains. Do you think they'd like that?"

"Gee, that'd be great. And Aunt Vic can take on that Joey Heaten. He thinks he's great at playing video games."

"You betcha," Aunt Vic agreed.

"Well, you can count on me as a chaperon," Danny said. "Right now I have to get into town, but I'd like to take you all to dinner tonight at the Inn, okay?"

They all agreed it would be a treat.

"Eh, Katherine," Mike said hesitantly after Danny had left. "Those guys down at the barbershop, I don't understand. They don't seem to like Danny very much, do they?"

Aunt Vic made a face. "They're just jealous because Danny has become successful. If they had any gumption, they'd get out and make something of themselves instead of playing games while they wait around for something that will never come."

Katherine glanced at her watch. She was running late for work. "Don't pay any attention to them, Mike. They're all stuck back in the 1700s. It's a miracle that there are still enough of them left to stage those silly war games.

* * *

Later, at the barbershop, she heard herself repeating that same phrase. "Fred, I understand that somebody in this group had some unkind things to say about Danny Dark, but I don't want to hear of it happening again. He is acting as a consultant to the mayor's office on this plant project, and I'd rather you not make him withdraw his support. There's been too much discord already."

"Maybe so," Fred said grudgingly, "but I don't trust Danny. At least his daddy never pretended to be something he wasn't. Danny was always trouble. Now you want us to listen to him tell us how to build a factory that's going to bring in more people just like those no-account Darks?"

"Yeah," a chorus of voices agreed.

"I don't believe what I'm hearing," Katherine spouted angrily. "Just look around on the street outside. How many children do you see? How many babies?"

Not many was the consensus of opinion. "So?" they asked.

"So how do you expect this town to continue to exist. There was a time when Dark River was considered a desirable place to live. But our town is shrinking. The population is getting older, and the younger people are moving out."

"Nah," Fred argued. "Our population stays about the same."

"Yes, but only because the people moving in are retired, looking for a quiet place to live. They live on fixed incomes that don't allow for increased taxes. Where do we get the funds to maintain what we have? Don't you see, we're stagnating just like the river swamp."

Katherine left the game-playing men with their mouths open. She hadn't put her concern into words so distinctly before, because she'd known that as mayor she should reflect the feelings of the taxpayers who wanted to maintain the status quo. But a manufacturing plant would generate new taxes and new people, too, and Dark River needed both.

Eventually the decision on the plant would be made. But the problem of Danny and Mike was becoming more complex than she'd ever dreamed. Danny had told her that he wanted to marry her and be a real father to Mike. But could she trust his sincerity? Was he still in love with her? If so, why had it taken him so long to come back and tell her?

How did she feel? The distance between them was the same from him to her as it was from her to him. It had taken a call from Aunt Vic, but he'd made the first attempt to bridge the gap. The next step was up to her—just as it always had been. There was Mike to consider, of course, but more than that, if they were to reach a workable solution, she had to resolve her doubts—all of them.

But a camping trip, with twenty nine-year-olds? She wasn't sure she was up to it.

First things first. A decision that was less traumatic but just as unsettling—what to wear to dinner? She turned to her closet.

Years before, she'd felt this same rush of excitement when she'd heard the sound of pebbles against her window. Danny would be signaling for her to join him in the garden. She'd slip down the stairs and into his arms. Even now she felt that same indescribable thrill. Danny was waiting.

Tonight they were going to dinner at the Inn. She finally chose a simple blue sundress with a soft, cross-stitched bodice and a flared skirt. She quickly ran a brush through her hair, picked up her purse, and headed downstairs.

"Aunt Vic, aren't you dressed?"

Victoria Willingham, still wearing her housedress, was stirring something on the stove.

"Oh, I'm sorry, Katherine, Mike and I aren't going. He isn't feeling too well."

"Oh, what's wrong? Have you called the doctor?"

"No. It's nothing serious. Just a sunburn and a little headache. Too much fun in the pool this afternoon. He's in his room, if you want to say good night. I'll keep an eye on him tonight."

Katherine turned and ran up the stairs. After a quick rap on the door, she went in. A suspicious rustle of paper under the pillow as she was entering was her first clue to the plotting of her aunt and her son. The clear absence of any appreciable flush on Mike's face confirmed her suspicions.

"Aunt Vic said that you weren't feeling well."

"Eh, yeah. I'm pretty sick."

"I see." She sat down on the bed. "Where does it hurt?"

"Hurt?" He cut a worried glance toward the door and then back to Katherine. "It . . . it's a stomachache."

"From eating all those peaches this afternoon, huh?"

"Yeah, all those peaches. I guess Aunt Vic and I can't go to dinner with you and Danny."

"Well, we'll miss you. I understand that the Inn has a special tonight on strawberry shortcake."

Mike bit back a look of envy and lifted his eyes as Aunt Vic came inside with a tray. "I brought you some chicken soup, Mike. Katherine, Danny's waiting downstairs."

"Chicken soup? I thought we were going to have pizza."

"Get the pizza, Aunt Vic," Katherine said as she left the room. She peered back around the door frame and added, "It ought to be just what Mike needs for a peach overdose."

Katherine smothered a laugh as she watched her aunt and Mike look at each other in confusion, then continued down the stairs.

"I like the sound of that. An evening that begins with a laugh can only get better." Danny stood nonchalantly at the bottom of the steps. "Where is everybody?" he asked.

"Mike's being sick."

"What's wrong?" Danny started up the steps in alarm.

"Nothing, except I think they're waiting for us

to get out of the house so he can get well enough to have pizza."

"I'm not sure I understand."

"Neither do I, not yet, but I'm beginning to. Our son and my aunt are plotting to get us alone together. What do you think about that?"

"I think I'll just go up and say good night."

Katherine followed behind, staying just out of sight in the hallway while Danny went inside.

"Katherine says you're not feeling well, Mike."

"Eh, yes, I have a—stomachache."

"He has a—sunburn," Aunt Vic said at the same time.

"Okay, you guys, what's going on up here?" Danny leaned against the door frame and waited.

"Well, Danny," Mike answered, "the way I see it, Aunt Vic and I think that Katherine needs a good man, and we've decided that you're him."

"Oh, you think so, do you? And how did you arrive at that conclusion?"

There was a silence before Mike began. "Seriously, Danny, I know how hard it's going to be on Katherine, taking care of me. Lots of men wouldn't understand. I talked it over with Aunt Vic and we—I decided that even if you did have to travel around to be successful, I wouldn't mind your being gone, if Katherine doesn't."

"I see. And how do you two think I should bring this about?"

"Hell, Danny, I mean, well heck, if a man wants a woman, he ought to go after her, don't you think?"

Katherine's heart swelled. It was all she could

do not to run into the room and hug all three of them. Instead she turned and slipped quietly away. When Danny came back down the stairs, she was waiting on the porch, fanning her flushed face with one of Aunt Vic's paper fans.

"What do you think about Mike's sickness?"

"I believe," he answered quietly, "that we have two very smart relatives. I think we'll keep them."

Danny stared at her in the twilight. He'd been sure that staying with Katherine and Mike was the right thing to do. What the future would bring wasn't as easy to sort out. He wished he knew what she was thinking, standing there so solemnly in the half shadows, her blue eyes wide with uncertainty. What he wanted to do was gather her up in his arms, take her across the yard into the guest house, and make love to her. She might not still be in love with him, but she wasn't indifferent to him. She wanted him, too.

"Well, Mr. Dark," she finally said in a rush, "what I think is that I'm hungry. What are you going to feed me?"

He reached out and grazed her cheek with his fingertip. "How'd you feel about feasting on moonbeams showered with stardust."

Katherine dropped the fan and caught her breath. "Better make that a double order, I'm famished."

"Shall we start with the main course," he whispered as he nibbled at the corners of her mouth, "or go straight for dessert?"

"I'll leave it up to you," she whispered, "I think, if Aunt Vic has her way, we have all night."

Six

The Inn was softly lit with cream-colored candles. Cut glass candlesticks became crystal prisms showering rainbow circles across the tablecloth.

The din of conversation died down for a moment as Katherine and Danny walked into the restaurant and waited to be seated by their host. After a resigned lifting of his eyebrow, Joe led Danny and Katherine across the dining room to a corner table overlooking the river. A wave of muted whispers followed them.

"I hope you enjoy your meal," Joe said with a tight smile, handing each of them a menu. He paused as if he wanted to say more, then, nodding, he wheeled around and was gone.

"Well," Katherine said, "that's not the most enthusiastic greeting I've ever had. Do you suppose he expected a tip?"

"Maybe he wanted to hit me," Danny countered. "You know he's still in love with you."

Katherine spoke softly. "I know, and I'm sorry."

"He always was. If you knew how many times he

threatened me with various broken limbs—and worse."

"Joe is a good person," Katherine admitted, "but we could never be more than friends. He knows that. He's always known how I felt about you."

The waiter, who introduced himself as Andrew, arrived to inquire about drink orders. Danny ordered beer. Katherine selected iced tea with lemon. Andrew left them with the promise to return after they had a chance to make their dinner selections.

In the background a band played soft music. An occasional laugh trilled across the room like the notes of a flute. Katherine realized that she was holding her open menu without having read a word of its offerings. Danny made no pretense of even cracking his. He simply stared across the table with a gaze so intense, she felt for a moment that he could see inside her.

"Do you realize, Katherine Sinclair, that this is the first time we've ever had a real official date, out in public, before God and everybody?"

"Yes, I guess it is. Are you enjoying being on parade?"

"Hell, no," he said with a growl. "I'd rather be sitting on the riverbank eating cupcakes and drinking soda."

"Well, we're not. And it would probably be a good idea not to look as if you want to . . . to . . ."

"Kiss you silly? Can't help it. It's out in the open now for all the world to see. Ah, Katherine, do you suppose that just for tonight we could forget about everything and enjoy ourselves?"

"I'd like that, Danny. I'd like that very much."

"Fine." He stood and pulled her up. "Let's dance."

The postage-stamp dance floor was filled, forcing Katherine tightly into Danny's arms. She was grateful for the dim lighting. She badly needed to hide the dreamy expression she was sure marked her face.

Danny was a smooth dancer, guiding her effortlessly with his hands and his body. They fit together, her softness cushioning his strength, her heart echoing the thundering of his more powerful beats, her breathing perfectly synchronized with his.

When the music ended, Danny led her back to the table. He seemed reluctant to release her. "You know, don't you," he whispered as he pushed her chair beneath the table, "that Danny Dark still has a crush on Katherine Sinclair."

"I think so." Her voice was unsteady, her pulse still racing wildly.

He sat down opposite her. "I feel . . . no, I started to say fourteen, but that's wrong. I feel at least seventeen again. Will you go steady with me, Katherine Sinclair?"

He didn't look seventeen. With his dark hair rakishly mussed from the ride in the open convertible and eyes that sizzled with sensuality, he was the man of every woman's dream.

Dare she put aside her doubts and enjoy their evening together? Yes. Tonight he was hers.

Tonight she could play, too, and pushing aside the last of her reservations, she fell readily into the lighthearted playacting, replying impishly, "only if I can wear your class ring."

"Sorry, princess, I never got one of those. Will this do?" He dislodged the napkin from the silver holder in the center of the plate and took Katherine's hand in his.

"Don't you think it's a little gaudy, perhaps a bit too large?"

"No, it's just right. It's big enough for all your fingers. I'm claiming your entire hand." He enclosed her fingers with the silver ring and lifted them to his lips for a kiss. "This makes us official," he whispered throatily. "I'll stake my claim on the rest of you later."

"Don't you think it makes us a bit obvious," Katherine said softly. But she didn't make any attempt to draw back her hand.

"I don't mind, if you don't."

"I don't. There's just one thing, Danny."

"What?"

"Andrew, our waiter. He's come to take our order. I think we're holding him up."

Danny turned his head slowly. "I tell you what, Andrew. You go back to the kitchen and bring us whatever you think we'd enjoy. I just don't want to be interrupted for any reason. In other words, I don't want to know you're here, understand?"

"Eh, yes, sir," the boy stammered.

"Oh, and one last thing," Danny called the boy back and with his finger beckoned him to bend down so he could whisper in his ear. "Do you think you can handle that?"

"Yes, sir!" The boy beamed, tucking a folded bill discreetly into his pocket. "I think I can handle that just fine."

"What was that all about?" Katherine inquired curiously.

"Nothing for you to be concerned about, my dear. Tonight Danny Dark is courting his girl, and she's just agreed to wear his ring. Anything else is for later. Are you happy, Katherine?"

Happy? Yes, she was happy. This was a wonderful evening, the kind she'd always dreamed about, but underneath the playacting she pushed down the knowledge that this wasn't real. Being there with Danny was a beautiful fantasy, and fantasies always ended. In spite of her best effort she knew he could see the flicker of doubt in her eyes. "What's wrong, princess?"

"Wrong? Nothing is wrong now," she teased. "It's your claiming the rest of me later that has me worried."

"Not to worry, Katherine, this is our night. We're going to make up for what we've missed. I promise you."

And they did. They ate and danced and talked, oblivious to the other patrons who came and went, until at last Joe strolled over to the table and stood for a moment before clearing his throat.

"I'm sorry, guys, but everybody has gone, and we need to clean up."

Katherine glanced around in surprise. All the

other candles had been blown out. The tables were cleared and set for tomorrow, and she and Danny were alone in their corner of the darkened restaurant.

"Sorry, Joe," Danny said, coming to his feet. "I didn't realize we were holding you up."

"No problem, Dan, it's happened before."

Danny left a handful of crumpled-up bills on the table and gathered Katherine into the curve of his arm as they followed Joe to the door. "Thanks, Joe, for everything."

"Yeah, sure. Hey, Andrew said you were to have this on the way out." He reached behind the bar and handed Danny a paper bag that clinked as he took it.

Only the muted lights recessed in the trees were still lit as Katherine and Danny walked along the river back to the car.

"This evening has been very special, Danny," Katherine said softly. "Thank you."

"That sounds like good night. No way, princess. You just hold on, you ain't seen nothing yet." He assisted her into the convertible from the driver's side, slid in behind her, and swept her into his arms.

"Oh, Lord, Katherine, I've wanted to do this all night. Being together in public is pure hell. I didn't know how much I missed you." He wasn't simply holding her, he was rocking her back and forth, threading his fingers through her hair in some kind of desperate gesture of reassurance.

She felt the tension in his grip, as though his nerves and muscles were stretched so tight they were about to snap.

"I'm so sorry," he murmured. "Can you ever forgive me?"

Nuzzling her cheek against his chest, she began to whisper over and over again, "It's all right, Danny. It's all right. You didn't do anything."

"Yes, I did," he said in a very quiet, very sad voice. "After all the times you stood by me, when you needed me most, I left you."

"Yes, but you came back when you thought I needed you. Don't you see, that makes everything all right."

He loosened the steel grip he had on her. The tinkle of glass reminding them both that he was still holding the bag Andrew had left for them. He suddenly laughed, and she felt the stiffness ease from his body.

"Maybe," he agreed, planting a light kiss on her lips, "but I'm not sure you ought to let me off that easy. Maybe I ought to be tarred and feathered."

"No, I'm into other kinds of torture, Danny Dark. For now, I think I'll just hold you to your promise. Remember, there's still the rest of me." She held up her hand. Her fingers were encased by the silver napkin ring.

"You stole the napkin ring?" Danny chuckled. "I'm engaged to a thief."

"I think you set me up, all the way, big guy. Can I expect Joe to have me arrested for theft?"

"I think that Joe would give you the whole restaurant, if you wanted it," Danny said, sliding the paper bag behind the seat and reaching into his pocket for the keys. "But me? That may be another story. I think I have to teach you to set a better example for our son."

"Good! Do I get private lessons?"

The engine caught and Danny eased the car into reverse. At the exit he turned back to Katherine, his voice hesitant as he said, "About staking my claim to the rest of you, my emotions always outrun my head when we're together. I've already gone down one wrong road, Katherine. I don't know where this one is going, but I don't want to make that mistake again."

"I'm traveling with you, Danny. Maybe I'll give the directions this time."

"Are you sure, Katherine?"

And at that moment all doubt fell away. She was still in love with him, completely, utterly. And that love had to be the basis of the direction for the rest of her life. She might have followed blindly once, but now she was choosing with her mind and her heart. "I'm very sure, Danny."

"All right, where do we go from here?"

"To the river, Danny Dark. According to my watch, it's just about midnight."

She slid across the seat and into the curve of his arm as he pressed the gas pedal to the floor. The night air caught her hair and tousled it, blowing a strand across his face. "Oops, I'm sorry," she said, winding her arm behind her neck and pulling her hair behind her ear.

"No, I like it touching me. I like you touching

me. Everything about you touching me makes me feel brand-new."

Katherine put her hand on his thigh and felt the ripple of his muscles beneath her touch.

"Are you cold?" she asked innocently, rubbing the spot that twitched.

"Cold? No, darling. I'm on fire."

Katherine smiled and leaned her head against his shoulder. She understood. She, too, felt the wanting and wondered how this one man could fill her body with such heat and her life with such joy.

Overhead the moon was high, casting a silver sheen across the countryside. Katherine felt as if they were the only two people in the world.

At the river Danny retrieved a blanket from the trunk. Placing it under his arm, he lifted the bag from behind the seat and opened Katherine's door.

"Shall we, my princess?"

"Shall we what?"

"Feast on moonlight and us, together again?"

"Oh, yes, Danny." She slid out, took his hand, and danced down the path to the river.

"It's still the same," she said in a low whisper.

They were standing in a secluded circle beneath an oak tree at the river's edge. Great wisps of moss hung from the limbs creating a fine curtain. Beyond the tree, the water, dark and mysterious, rippled musically along on its seaward journey.

"Katherine, come and sit down."

Danny had spread the blanket on the ground. He was sitting cross-legged in the darkness. The tinkling of glass reminded her of the puzzling gift left by the waiter at the Inn.

Katherine swayed, an unexpected shyness sweeping over her. This had been their secret place. They'd come there to hide from the world and be together. It hadn't mattered that they were both two lonely children seeking the love that was denied them at home. It hadn't mattered that Danny's father had been an alcoholic and that Katherine's father never had had any time for his child. She and Danny had been each other's shelter from the storm.

Tonight they faced that storm openly. And everything felt right. Why, then, did she suddenly turn shy and uncertain? This was Danny, her Danny, who'd come home again because he thought she needed him. He was right. She did.

"What's wrong, Katherine? Are you having second thoughts about us?"

"About us, here together? No, no second thoughts, Danny." She dropped down to the blanket beside him. "About our future, perhaps."

"Then, don't think about our future, Katherine. Remember, we've already been lost, and we've managed to get back on track again. This time we're making ourselves a map, right after we have our snack."

"Our snack? After all that food at the restaurant you ordered more food?"

She heard him open the bag. There was a crinkle of cellophane and the unmistakable pop of a soft drink bottle cap being opened.

"That's right. Hold out your hand."

Katherine complied, expecting to feel a bottle being placed in her fingers. She didn't. What she got was a warm kiss followed by a small iced cake. "What is it, Danny?"

"Take a bite and see."

She did, tasting the rich dark chocolate and creamy filling. "Cupcakes. Oh, Danny, I can't believe it. You ordered cupcakes from the restaurant?"

"Cupcakes and—"

This time the object he handed her *was* a bottle and this time she knew. "Danny, how did you manage this? I happen to know that Joe does not stock cupcakes and soda pop in his restaurant."

"Nope, but the Big Town Market down the road does, and Andrew got special permission to fill a take-out order."

Katherine succumbed to the magic of moonlight and memories. Eating cupcakes and drinking lukewarm soda with Danny was simply wonderful. All her doubts were washed away. When he tugged at her hand, she responded by lying down beside him, her head on his arm, their fingers laced together and resting on his chest.

For a long time they lay, absorbing the familiar warmth of each other's body, measuring their uneven breathing and pulses.

"Do you remember the first time we did this?" Danny finally asked.

Katherine closed her eyes. "Do you mean the first time we came to the river or the first time we lay down side by side?"

"I mean the first time we touched each other, the first time I did this." He raised up on his elbow so that he was leaning over her, his other hand still entwined with hers. He slid their hands higher, grazing her breasts with his fingertips. The heat from his touch burned through her sundress top.

"Yes," she said with a gasp. "I thought I'd die."

He wiggled his fingers loose and began to untie the strings holding the dress on her shoulders. "You were so still, I could feel your heartbeat, fluttering beneath my hand like the wings of a frightened bird."

"You mean something like now?"

He laid his hand on her chest, pressing down against nipples jutted like firm cherries against the sensitive skin of his palm. He held still for a long moment, then spread his fingers to encompass and lift up her bare breast. He heard a sharp intake of breath and didn't know whether it was hers or his.

"Something like now," he repeated in a ragged voice, letting his head fall forward. He took her mouth, slowly, leisurely, letting the bliss of their kiss catch fire and melt the last of their resistance. Like tasting a fine wine, he sipped at her, invaded her mouth and with his tongue, extracted every dewy ounce of her loving elixir.

Katherine didn't question her feelings any further. When he pulled his lips away, feathering his tongue down her body to her breast, she thrust her chest forward seeking the intoxicating heat of his mouth.

He licked and suckled and pulled on her until she was writhing with wanting. It was beyond anything she had ever felt or dreamed of. Danny undressed her, then himself, covering her with his body, setting her on fire with his teasing. Each time she reached for him, snuggled closer, he pulled back, building her desire.

At last he lifted himself over her and gripped her shoulders. She was so ready for him to love her that she moaned when he lifted himself completely away from her.

"Danny, please, I want you. Don't stop now."

He gave a low, wicked laugh. "That's not what you used to say, my darling."

"Yes, and you didn't pull away from me then."

"I know, and I should have. But I was too young, and I loved you too much. This time I want to take care of you."

"Oh." Take care of her. She'd been so aroused that she hadn't thought. Fire burned across her face, but it was swallowed up in the heat that shot through her as he laid himself back against the vee between her legs. Cupping the heaviness of her swollen breasts once more in his hand, he touched his lips to her, taking little nibbles, planting quick kisses, all the while sliding himself up and down, fanning her passion to heights that she'd never reached before.

Her hands tangled in the thickness of his hair, her breath caught in her tight throat. "Please, Danny," she gasped. "If you don't hurry, I shall die."

"Then I won't wait any longer," he whispered, "for I don't want to lose you now."

Katherine arched her back, opening herself up for him, moaning softly, her breathing coming faster as she felt the last shreds of control slip away.

"Nothing's changed, Katherine. You're still mine. You always will be." His mouth recaptured hers. His hands slid beneath her hips and lifted her to meet the hard length of his arousal. There was nothing gentle about his loving, and she met him thrust for thrust until she gave one last cry of release and fell to the ground in sated silence.

"Oh, Danny," she whispered, then wiggled her body for a moment before it registered that he was still hard inside her. "Is something wrong?"

"Nothing's wrong," he whispered, concentrating with all his strength on icebergs and snowstorms. He'd waited for ten years to love Katherine again, and he was determined to make it last.

After being very still for what seemed to be a very long time, he began to move again, slowly this time, sweetly. He covered her face with kisses, caressed her breasts with the mat of hair on his chest, ground himself against her until she was quivering, too.

He lifted himself slightly and slid one hand between them so that he could touch her while he rocked back and forth, coaxing, demanding, until she couldn't hold back any longer.

She cried out in wonder as she felt the heat inside her spill over in rippling waves of ecstasy that exploded in the intensity of Danny's release.

"Together, Katherine," he murmured, "the way we were meant to be."

When he finally fell away in exhaustion, he curled Katherine to him, holding her so that she was half-lying across his body.

"Too bad the world doesn't know our secret, darling," he whispered into her hair.

"What secret?" she asked in alarm.

"Cupcakes and soda," he admitted solemnly. "Think what its application would mean to medical research."

"Oh? Are we talking external or internal?" Contentedly she snuggled against him.

"Hadn't thought about external application," Danny admitted, then raised himself up and reached for the paper bag. "But say, there's more in the bag. I'm game if you are."

The house was dark when they drove up the long drive. Pale fingers of light streaked the horizon, and the early morning call of the birds filled the air.

Once he'd stopped the car, Danny turned back, pulling Katherine into his arms again. There was a desperate urgency about his grasp, as if he were afraid that once she was inside the house she'd be lost to him forever.

"Come to the guest house with me," he whispered.

"No, Danny, we can't. What about Mike?"

"Mike's in the house with Aunt Vic. Why do you

think she set up that illness story? So that we could be together."

"We have been for most of the night."

"But it's still not open and honest, is it?" Danny turned her face up so that he could see her eyes. Even in the darkness he could see her concern.

"You want us to be together in front of Mike? How would that look to an impressionable boy?"

"The way two parents ought to look together, as if they love each other, as if they love their son."

"But, Danny, Mike doesn't know that we're his parents. And we aren't married."

"We could fix that. We could get married and both problems would be solved. We belong together, Katherine. We always have."

Yes, Katherine wanted to say, *I believe you. But I believed you before and you left. And you'll leave again. It's just a matter of time.*

A chill ran down her spine, and she forced herself from his arms. "Oh, Danny, let's not talk about that. Let's take it one step at a time. It's late. I'd better go inside." Quickly Katherine got out of the car and started toward the porch.

"I take it this is a no?" he said from the darkness behind her.

Her voice came back in a low whisper. "Let's just say that I've filed your request under pending. Go to bed, Danny. I have to work tomorrow."

"The pending file. I like that. Good night, my Katie. I'll meet you in my dreams."

Meet you in my dreams, the words Danny

always whispered in her ear when they'd said good night. *Katie.* Me and you, Katie, he'd say. Tonight he hadn't said that he loved her, but he'd called her Katie. Halfway up the stairs she turned around and started back across the yard. Halfway to the guest house she met Danny heading her way.

"I had a handful of rocks," he confessed as he showered her with kisses.

"Shush! What did you plan to do with them?"

"I thought I'd throw them at your window until you came back to me."

"Oh, Danny, I don't want this night to end either, but I don't feel right about being with you here."

"You're right, princess. I understand. That's why we're going to take a moon bath." He picked her up and carried her to one of the lounge chairs by the pool, holding her close beside him.

"A moon bath," she said, relaxing against him with a satisfied yawn. "How nice. I don't know why somebody hasn't thought of this before."

"Neither do I, seems like a darned good idea to me." His kiss was tender. His arms were warm. Katherine snuggled as close as she could get. The last thing she remembered was seeing a shooting star flash across the night sky. The last thing she heard was Danny whispering love words in her ear.

For the rest of the week it was like the last days before Christmas—secret whispers, stolen kisses, and tender glances. Between the four of them it was difficult to tell who was the kid and who was guarding the biggest surprise.

Katherine and Danny and Mike. It felt right for them to be together. Mike seemed to be on the same emotional wavelength as Danny was, and that made it easy for Katherine to anticipate his reactions. More and more Mike was becoming a part of their lives. He seemed to need to stay close. One morning when Danny was busy, Mike even asked if he could go to work with her.

Katherine was surprised but pleased.

"If that's a bad idea, forget it," Mike blurted out, and started to turn away. "I just thought it would be neat to see what you do."

"I think that's a fine idea," Katherine agreed enthusiastically. "As a matter of fact, I have a little chore to take care of, and you're just the one to do it."

"Really? Just you and me?" Mike's face brightened and he tore into his breakfast. "And I won't have to wait in the park?"

Wait in the park? Just you and me? Katherine was stunned. Is that what Mike thought, that he was in the way?

"Of course you won't have to wait in the park, Mike. Finish your breakfast, and we'll go."

"Eh, Danny," Aunt Vic interceded, "what are you up to today?"

"Well, I've found some interesting references to the original Dark land grant, but I can't be sure how accurate my information is. I'm going to run into town and have some title checks run. Then I'll know."

Aunt Vic stood behind Mike's chair, her hand resting on his shoulder. "How exciting. I hope you aren't disappointed, Danny. Dark River's past is supposed to be pretty shady."

"Oh, I'm reasonably sure I know all I need to know about the land. It's the people who settled it I'm not sure about. One thing I've learned recently, nothing is as simple as it seems."

Katherine felt his gaze on her. She lifted her eyes and for a second they seemed connected. This, too, was happening with increasing frequency. She could feel him, feel him searching, groping for answers. Then they'd focus on each other and everything else disappeared. She smiled. He returned her smile.

"Oh, dear," Aunt Vic muttered in mock despair. "Mike, I think you'd better help me clear the table. These two are off in space again."

"What?" Mike turned to Aunt Vic with a frown, caught her smile and the shake of her head, and gave her a conspiratorial grin in return. "Eh, sure. Danny, are you eating that toast or smashing it?"

Danny glanced at the mangled crumbs of bread showering onto his plate and blushed. "Sorry, guess my mind was on something else."

"Yeah," Mike agreed, "I guess it was."

Thirty minutes later, Katherine and Mike were driving down River Road.

"Mike, I thought you might like to see the house where Danny lived when he was your age."

She turned off the main road and after a few minutes of cutting through streets that grew more and more seedy, she pulled up before one old house and stopped.

"Danny lived here?" Mike asked, eyeing the ramshackle house with the porch that had long since fallen in and the roof that was patched with assorted strips of roofing and oilcloth.

"Yes, he did."

"Yeah, but it probably didn't look like this then, did it?"

"Pretty much," Katherine admitted. "His father was a nice man, but he had a drinking problem. Some people said that he lost the woman he loved and never got over it. I don't know. Nobody ever knew Danny's mother. I just know that Mr. Dark wasn't able to provide much of a home for his son. I think that's why it's so important to Danny to succeed."

"His dad should have let him be adopted like me," was Mike's practical observation.

"Maybe his mother wouldn't give him up."

"Maybe she didn't love him like my real mother loved me."

Like my real mother loved me. Katherine didn't know why she'd brought Mike to see Danny's home. Perhaps it was because she knew that Danny could never explain the truth.

"Maybe she didn't, Mike. But that's why Danny works so hard, because he never wants to live like that again."

Mike stared at the house. "That's why he has to travel a lot, why he's going to that place—Saudi Arabia?"

"He told you he was leaving?"

"Yeah. I don't think he really wants to go. I think he'd rather stay here. My pop never went anywhere. He always had to run the store."

"Sometimes fathers have to be away, Mike, even if they'd rather not."

"Maybe. If Danny was my dad, I guess I'd understand, but I wouldn't like it. Katherine—" Perplexed, Mike chewed on his lower lip for a moment. "You came and got me when my mom and pop were killed. Did you know my real mother, I mean, when she was a little girl?"

"Yes, I knew her," Katherine answered quietly.

"Did she live in a place like this, too?"

No, the place she lived in wasn't like this, she almost said. But was it very different? she wondered. She tried not to think about the loneliness she felt growing up. But Mike's question brought it all back. Talking about herself hadn't been her intention when she'd agreed to allow Mike to accompany her, but maybe unconsciously she'd been waiting for him to ask. How was she to answer him?

"No, Mike," she finally said. "Your real mother lived in a very different kind of place. Her father wasn't like Danny's father, but he neglected her just as badly. She was very lonely and unhappy."

"Why?"

The question was so simple. The answer was much harder.

"I think because it really doesn't matter what kind of a house you live in or who your parents are. It's love, a loving family that matters. Your mother knew that, Mike. Your father was gone, and she couldn't give you a loving home. She . . . found someone who could—your adoptive parents."

"But my dad," Mike pressed the issue. "I don't understand how he could have left her."

He went away because he loved your mother so much. He thought he was doing the right thing by leaving her to a better life than he could give her."

"But he left me, too."

And he's already told you he's leaving again. That's what she wanted to say. But she couldn't. "He didn't know about you, Mike. I'm certain that one day he'll want to claim you, too. Just know that whatever happens, your mother loved you very much."

She'd have to wait. If Mike learned that she was his mother, Danny would want to tell him the rest. Mike knew he was adopted. He was handling that well. But how would he take learning that it had been Katherine who'd given him up? Katherine knew firsthand how it felt to be deserted. She knew the pain her father had caused with his rejection of her. What would happen if Mike decided that he'd rather live with Danny? She couldn't take the chance that Mike would choose to leave her. She put the car in gear.

"We'd better get to work. I'm expecting somebody to bring a book by my office this morning, and I think you might like to take a look at it."

"Book?" The enthusiasm died out of Mike's voice like air let out of a balloon.

"Oh, but this book should be very interesting, Mike. It's a diary kept during the Revolutionary War about what went on right here in Dark River. By the time you're finished reading it, you ought to be able to tell those guys down at the barbershop a thing or two they don't know about the Battle of Dark River."

"I will? *Alllll Riiiight.*"

Seven

"Whose diary is it, Katherine?" Mike asked.

"It belongs to Joe Hall now. You know the man who runs Dark River Inn? His family were some of the original settlers in the area, along with the Sinclairs. I told him about Danny's search for family history. He called yesterday and told me that in his family papers he'd found a copy of a very old diary that dates back nearly two hundred years. It belonged to his great-great-grandmother. He thought Danny might be interested in what she wrote."

"Ah, what would a woman have to say that would be important? Women didn't actually fight."

"Well, I don't know. But, personally, I'd love to read Amelia Earhart's diary. And what about Tokyo Rose or Anne Bonny?"

"Who are they?"

His question brought on a rousing discussion of the part women played in history.

"You know a lot for a girl," Mike finally conceded, a touch of admiration in his voice. My mother always talked to me as if I were just a kid. She was a teacher, you know."

Katherine felt a lump in her throat. "I know. You must miss her very much."

"Yeah, I guess, I do. But I like you pretty good, too, and Aunt Vic, and . . Danny."

Mike liked her too. Her world was just about complete. If only it could last, the three of them, she and Mike and Danny could be together.

By the time Katherine and Mike reached her office, Joe Hall had already left the diary with Nancy. Katherine settled Mike in a chair in the council room, giving him a magnifying glass and a tablet and cautioning him to be very careful with the old journal.

Closing the door, she hunted up Nancy. "What do you know about a camp-out this weekend? Was this, by any chance, your idea?"

"The Scout trip to the river? Why, are you going?"

"Aunt Vic volunteered my services."

"Somehow, boss, I don't think that comes under the heading of being mayor. I can't see you roughing it in the woods."

"What do you mean? Of course I can rough it. What exactly do you do?"

"For starters, we sleep on the ground."

"Oh." For a moment Katherine's mind flashed back to her weekend. A heated blush swept across her face. She was experienced, very experienced with being in the woods on the ground, though maybe she didn't know much about the sleeping part.

"In sleeping bags," Nancy quickly amended, her expression reflecting her confusion over Katherine's question. "Or in tents, or both."

"And what else do you do?"

"We mostly just keep them from killing themselves or each other. They're supposed to do the cooking and cleaning. I assume that you're bringing Mike?"

"Eh, yes. This trip is for Mike's benefit, to allow him to take part in summer activities with the other boys. But, Nancy, it's not just me. Aunt Vic volunteered Danny as a chaperon, too."

"Oh, I see. Aunt Vic's been plotting, has she? I knew she'd come up with something if you didn't."

"If I didn't? What do you mean, my suddenly shy secretary? Speak up, you've never been reticent before."

"Katherine, it's pretty plain that you and Danny have something going. It's also pretty plain that you wouldn't be going far without your aunt's maneuvering. You're such a turkey."

"Nancy Christopher, I'm perfectly capable of doing my own plotting. How dare you say such a thing. If I wanted Danny Dark, I'd go after him."

"Maybe, but you're moving along about as fast as an inchworm. And from what I hear, you only have about two weeks to get to the finish line."

"What do you mean?"

"Well, I know it's only gossip, and it probably doesn't mean anything, but according to Mary

Manley over at the travel agency, your Danny has booked a flight out of here the first of July—one way. If you intend to keep him here, you'd better get it in gear."

A flight? So why was that a problem? She'd known he had to go to Saudi Arabia. He'd told her that in the beginning. But he'd be back afterward, wouldn't he?

"Oh, I know about that trip, Nancy. He'll be back when he's finished with his meeting."

"Maybe, but he requested two tickets—two one-way tickets. Who's he taking with him?"

"I—" *Two* one-way tickets? He'd already said that he wanted to spend some time with Mike. Surely he wasn't planning to take Mike with him? It made no sense. The only thing she could understand was that Danny was leaving, that apparently he had no intention of returning.

"Stop holding your breath, Katherine. You're turning blue."

"Funny, that's more appropriate than you know," Katherine said, and turned back into her office.

Danny was leaving, without even discussing it with her. No matter that they'd made glorious, wonderful love; that they'd found each other again; that they seemed more right together now than they had ten years before. Danny was leaving.

So, he had told her in the beginning that he wouldn't be staying. He still had worlds to conquer. Dark River hadn't welcomed him back. It had been plain to him there was still no future for Danny Dark in this town. But she'd thought that had changed because of Mike. Danny had said that he wanted to be a father to their son. He'd wanted them to know each other again as adults, as parents to their child.

Well, they'd certainly done that. Her back had been pressed against every tree in the garden where they'd found a dark place for stolen kisses, and the lounge chairs by the pool had become shaped to their bodies from moonbathing after everyone else was in bed.

Danny and Mike were getting to know each other, too. So why was Danny leaving? Why hadn't he said anything? Because he didn't want her to know. Because nothing had really changed. Once, he'd swapped their love for a college degree and a chance at becoming a powerful, successful man. And he was doing the same thing again. The entire world had a prior claim on Danny Dark. She and Mike were in dismal second place.

The rest of the morning passed in a blur. Even Mike's excited discovery in the diary didn't erase her despair.

"Katherine, Katherine, look at this. She's talking a bunch of lovey, dovey stuff about a Captain Dark. He was a hero, a patriot. Fought the English. And guess what, he lived right here on the river."

Katherine forced herself to listen to Mike's revelation. "Probably one of Danny's relatives," she commented listlessly. It was suddenly hard for her to be interested in a revolution that occurred two hundred years before, when she was losing the battle in progress.

"And look, here's a Sinclair, too. 'Shotgun' Sinclair. Was that your relative?"

"So they say," Katherine agreed.

"But . . . Hey, Katherine, what does this mean? I can't read this word. It looks like lynch."

Katherine laid the shaft of papers she was studying down and sat at the table beside Mike. She might as well, she realized, she wasn't accomplishing anything.

Half an hour later Katherine closed the diary and let out a big sigh. The diary was astonishingly legible and complete, down to the last detail. What she'd just read was not only amazing, but, coupled with what Danny had already discovered in the town council minutes, could prove to be catastrophic to the city of Dark River.

"Let's hurry, Katherine. I can't wait to tell Danny that Dark River was the hideout for the Sinclair gang. Wow, can you believe that Shotgun Sinclair was really a Tory and that he got captured and hung by Captain Dark right out there in the city square?"

"No, that's hard to believe, Mike. In fact, I'm not sure that anybody will."

Mike jumped up and ran to the window. "I'll bet it happened right where that statue is."

Katherine couldn't keep back a smile. Mike didn't know, but that statue was a tribute to Samuel "Shotgun" Sinclair, who was supposed to be one of the heroes of the revolution and the founder of Dark River. That statue was a lie.

She started to laugh. For years her father had been more concerned with protecting the image of his family than in his only child. He'd sent Danny away to protect that reputation. Now, all these years later, Danny would be able to prove his point. Now the world would know the truth; Dark River truly belonged to Danny Dark.

All was won and all was lost. She gathered up the diary and Mike and went home. "I don't think I'll be back this afternoon, Nancy," she said with purpose in her voice. "I have some thinking to do."

But when they got home for lunch, Aunt Vic was the only one to learn Mike's news. Danny had gotten a phone call and had left, explaining that he'd be back in time for the camping trip. He'd left a note for Katherine.

Darling, be sure and stock up on cupcakes and soda for the weekend.

I love you, Katie.
Danny.

He'd finally acknowledged it. *I love you, Katie.* Even when they'd been seventeen, he'd never said he'd loved her. For the first time he'd told her, but he wasn't there for her to tell him that she loved him too.

The rest of the week passed slowly. Aunt Vic and Mike made endless lists, bought supplies, a

Scout uniform, and a tent. Katherine read and reread the diary.

There appeared to be no mistake. Old Shotgun Sinclair, under the guise of fighting for the mother country, stayed behind after every attack by the English and systematically looted every settler in the area. When the central government in Savannah sent Captain Daniel David Dark to find and arrest the culprit, he caught up with him and hung him on what was now the city square, thereafter giving that area the name Hangman's Hill.

The term Hangman's Hill was also used to describe the official grant given to Daniel David Dark after the Revolution, the grant that changed history and would likely change the future of Dark River as well.

The diary didn't explain how history had been rewritten. In the two hundred years since the event, the Darks and the Sinclairs had undergone a reversal of fortunes. They might never know the truth, but it was obvious that the statue in the park of old Shotgun Sinclair had been a big joke on somebody's part.

The problem with her and Danny wasn't so amusing. Half of her wanted to confront him and demand the truth about the one-way tickets. The other half of her wasn't so sure she wanted to force the issue. She still had two weeks. The only thing she was certain of was that she had Mike back, and she didn't intend to give him up again. In order to keep him she had to find a way to tell

Mike she was his mother. And that wasn't going to be an easy confession to make.

For now, Mike and Katherine decided to keep what they'd learned from the diary a secret. They needed to plan their disclosure for a time that would be most dramatic. It would be a glorious surprise for Danny when he returned.

Danny called on Thursday night. He talked to Mike for a moment, then Mike handed the phone to her.

"Hello, Katherine," he said in a voice that curled her toes and made her heart sing, even after she'd convinced herself that she wouldn't let him sweep her off her feet. "I've missed you."

"Did you have a good—trip?" she asked, trying not to let her indignation show.

"Methinks my lady is a bit piqued?" Danny said with a certain amount of pride. "She's missed me, even if she is pretending otherwise."

"I have not!" Her reply tumbled out before she could stop herself.

Danny smiled. He couldn't see her, but he could imagine how she looked, angry that he'd left and trying to keep her face stiff in the face of her crumbling resistance. Well, she wouldn't be able to hold out long. She'd soon change her mind when he showed her the ring he'd bought from the finest jeweler in Savannah, and the tickets he'd picked up for what he hoped would be their honeymoon.

"I just don't understand why you didn't let me

know what you were going to—what you were doing," she finished lamely. Why didn't she ask him straight out? She was no teenager now. If he was planning his departure, he owed it to her to come right out and say so. She might not like it, but she deserved to be treated with respect.

"Oh, I intend to tell you exactly what I have in mind. I'll be back tomorrow in time for the camping trip. After we have the guys settled down for the night, you and I are going to have a very long talk about the future. Once we get back from the woods, I have a surprise for you."

I'll bet, she wanted to say. *One-way tickets out of Dark River.* Instead she merely agreed, "Fine. I'll see you tomorrow afternoon."

Danny hung up the phone, puzzled at her lack of enthusiasm. Since they'd had dinner at Joe's, Katherine had instigated as many of their special moments as he. His research project had slowed to a snail's pace, and suddenly it hadn't mattered. So what, if the original land grant had given the Darks the land on which city hall and the square were located? He didn't need it. All he wanted was Katherine, and at last she seemed to be within his grasp.

But first he did have to deal with what he'd learned. For too many years he'd desperately needed to have roots. Now more than ever he wanted to be looked at as a success. Katherine deserved a man who was respected.

According to the minutes and his best advice, the time for free use of the land was up, and based on the law at the time the agreement was made, the city now had the option to buy the land at fair market value or return it to the heirs of Daniel David Dark—if Danny wanted to force the city's hand.

The land on which the plant would be located, if financing could be found, was another matter. A lawn furniture plant was a small thing, but it was a good investment, and whether the city fathers understood it or not, it would be good for Dark River. Giving something to Dark River that would really be beneficial to the citizens appealed to Danny. If he could just convince the city council that he knew his business.

In truth, after listening for two days to the best legal advice he could buy in Savannah, there was nothing they could do to stop him if he wanted to claim all the land. However, Danny thought that they might be open to a compromise. He'd give city hall and the square to them outright, and he'd keep the land on which his family had always lived. He smiled to himself. His daddy had been right all along. Dark River did belong to the Darks, and now the world would know the truth, once and for all.

"You don't mean we're taking all this?" Danny glanced at the stack of supplies in the foyer and shook his head. "This is a camp-out, not a world cruise."

"I know, Danny, but you try and tell these women that."

Mike was wearing a smart new green uniform,

stiff new hiking boots, and knee socks that made him look like something straight out of a Norman Rockwell painting.

Danny pursed his lips and gave his son a big wink. "Well . . . that's why they kept ladies out of the Boy Scouts in the first place. You really can't expect them to rough it."

"Now, just a minute," Katherine argued, wondering why she was allowing herself to respond to a man who was probably already packing his own travel bags. "I can do anything you two can do, and probably better."

"Shades of Annie Oakley," Danny said with a grin as he walked over and pulled Katherine into his arms. "Hello, Katherine. I'm glad I'm home."

He kissed her. It was a light, hello kind of kiss. Still, Katherine gasped. Danny had kissed her in front of Aunt Vic and Mike! She was standing there, eyes wide, heart pounding, being held in Danny's arms with everybody watching. Her mouth fell open in total disbelief.

When he kissed her the second time, it wasn't light and it wasn't subtle.

Mike cleared his throat and said an embarrassed, "Ah, you guys. Why don't you go someplace else? You're blocking the door, and I need to load the car."

"No time for courtin' now," Aunt Vic interrupted. "Danny, you're on the tent-raising committee. Go get your clothes changed while we pack the car. Katherine, stop kissing Danny and give us a hand."

Dazed, Katherine pulled herself from Danny's

arms and watched as he strode toward the guest house, stopping only to pick up his overnight bag and blow Katherine a kiss.

"Be with you in a minute," he said in a low voice. "You two climb in."

Mike began to lug the supplies to Danny's car, carefully loading the tall items in the back and the rest of the gear in the trunk.

Katherine, who was still standing in the hall, watched Danny disappear past the pool.

"What's wrong, Katherine?" Victoria asked, smothering a grin. "You having trouble going public?"

"Oh, Aunt Vic, it isn't the way it looks. He's leaving me," she replied stiffly.

"Only temporarily, my dear, he'll be back in two shakes."

"No, I mean really. The girl down at the travel agency says that he's already bought his plane ticket. He's leaving in two weeks."

Victoria Willingham took Katherine's shoulders in her hands and shook her. "Now listen here, girl. Danny Dark loves you. He always has. And you love him. I don't believe for one minute that he's going to leave you unless you let him do it. You may not have been old enough to know how to hold a man when you were seventeen, but you've had ten years to live with regret. Don't be a fool. Find a time to talk to him about the future while you're out in the woods. You can stop him if you're tough enough."

All the way to the river Katherine let Aunt Vic's words run round and round in her mind. Danny seemed to be unusually happy, singing songs and joking with his son. Between them, Mike was jabbering with excitement. He'd accepted their kiss as natural and right.

"Katherine's awfully quiet, Mike. I think that she's worried about camping out. But we'll take care of her, won't we?"

"Sure," Mike agreed readily.

"I am not worried," Katherine snapped. "It's just that I don't know why you want me here. This trip is for men and I'm a woman."

"A definite fact," Danny agreed, sliding his arm along the back of the seat so that he could touch her. "I love your . . . whatever it is you're wearing."

"It's a sunsuit, and I can't say I care much for whatever it is you're wearing."

Danny looked down at his camouflage pants and boots. They were faded, but appropriate for the trip ahead of them. He very much doubted that Katherine had any idea what she'd let herself in for. A three-mile hike in that sunsuit was going to be rough on her bare skin. At least she was wearing sneakers.

"Danny looks like Rambo," Mike said. "He's cool. Aunt Vic said to tell you that she put a pair of jeans and a shirt in your backpack, Katherine."

"My backpack?" Katherine was beginning to get a bad feeling about what was coming. She'd been so concerned after learning about the one-way tickets that she'd paid little attention to the plans for the trip.

"Well, we have to carry all our stuff, and hiking is easier if you carry your gear on your back."

"What do you mean, hiking? I thought we were going to camp by the river and build a fire. Nancy said we'd sleep in a tent and that you guys would cook."

"Sure," Mike explained. "But the campsite is three miles upriver. And we have to get there first."

"If you want to turn back," Danny volunteered, "you can drop us off and take the car. We'd understand. It does take a tough woman to hold her own with us guys."

Tough, Katherine thought, that's what Aunt Vic had said. If she was tough enough. Well, she didn't know what Danny had in mind, but Katherine Sinclair could make plans, too. And as of right now, she intended to make very sure that the father of her child was going to have a hard time leaving Dark River.

Katherine took one look at the dare in Danny's eyes and gritted her teeth. "No, thanks, Danny. I'm looking forward to this weekend, and a three-mile hike sounds just fine."

An hour later she was having grave doubts about even reaching the campsite. The Scouts and their leaders were strung out along the trail that wound beside the river. She and Danny and Mike were the last ones in the line. Danny and Mike strode forward, seemingly oblivious to the briars that came out of nowhere to snare her ankles. Little black stinging insects danced frantically about her face and bare shoulders. The mascara she was wearing definitely wasn't perspiration proof; her eyes stung, and she couldn't reach a tissue, even if she'd had one. Her head ached, and the metal contraption they'd strapped on her back felt as if it weighed two hundred pounds.

But what was worse, Danny seemed not to notice. He was involved with Mike, sharing his excitement and marching on without a backward glance. She sighed and tried to hurry. But there was no use. How could she possibly expect to stop Danny from leaving Dark River when she couldn't even stop him from leaving her on a hiking trail?

Then suddenly she looked up and realized that she'd fallen behind. The hikers had disappeared from sight and she was alone. They'd left the riverbank somewhere back down the trail, and she had no idea which way to go. Katherine slid the pack off her shoulders and sat down on the stump of a tree, a tear rolling down her cheek.

They'd left her. They didn't even know she was gone. She was just a piece of unwelcome baggage. Why on earth had she thought this was a good idea. She was about as out of place in the woods as she would be in Paris, or wherever it was Danny was heading. She was just a diversion for Danny, a rest stop between his trips.

"Damn you, Danny Dark. You always were a con man!"

"Absolutely! Good idea, darling." Danny was suddenly beside her, sliding his own pack from his shoulders. "I couldn't think of a way to get you alone. Smart move on your part, pretending not to be able to keep up."

He was pulling her into his arms. He was hot, sticky, and unmistakably aroused.

"Danny, what do you think you're doing?"

"I'm loving my lady," he replied, and caught her lips with his own.

Her angry, "But—" was cut off by his breathless assault on her senses. For a few minutes she forgot what she'd been about to say, and Danny forgot where they were. It was Mike's voice down the trail that finally brought them back to reality.

"Hey, Danny. Did you find her? Is she all right?"

"She's perfect, Mike. Go on with the others, we'll catch up as soon as Katherine rests for a minute."

But it wasn't rest that Danny had in mind. And Katherine's mind simply wasn't functioning at all. It went blank the moment he touched her, and for the next thirty minutes, it simply refused to reactivate at all.

When they finally reached the campsite, Mike was unrolling his sleeping bag and clearing a space for the tent Danny had brought along for Katherine. Nancy wandered over and casually said, "Good move, kid, you probably won't get another opportunity to be with the big guy until tomorrow."

Katherine gasped. She was doing a lot of that lately. She stood around stupidly, trying not to feel as if everybody were staring at her. The stinging insects were soon replaced by mosquitoes that could have carried off the statue of Shotgun Sinclair. Katherine slapped at her arms and legs until she was totally miserable.

After erecting Katherine's tent and laying out Mike's sleeping bag next to his own bag, Danny turned to help build a giant campfire in the middle of the clearing. As the sun began to set they laid rock around the site, burned off a safe buffer zone, and demonstrated to the Scouts the proper way to stack the wood for the fire.

Danny was good with Mike and the other boys. If anyone resented his presence, Katherine couldn't tell. Katherine felt a warm feeling steal over her. She and Danny and Mike were on an outing by Dark River, just as if they were really a family.

Finally Katherine gave up any pretense of taking part and retreated to the tent, where she could zip herself away from the insects. Feeling completely rotten, she gave up and faced the reality of the moment. She was a total mess.

She retrieved the jeans and shirt that Aunt Vic had packed, along with a towel and soap, and slipped away in the twilight. There was a cooking demonstration being conducted at the fire. Nobody would miss her, and if she didn't get clean, she was going to die. She found her way to the river and looked for a secluded spot away from the camp. Quickly she slid her soiled sunsuit from her body and waded out.

The water felt heavenly. It was cool and soothing to her ravished skin. She washed herself and her hair, ducking her head back in the swift moving water to rinse it. A sound from the bank caught her attention and she stopped.

"Is someone there?"

"Yes, ma'am. There most certainly is. Are you standing up out there?"

It was Danny. He'd come after her. "Yes, I'm standing up."

"You're sure the water isn't over your head? You're touching the bottom?"

"No, the water isn't over my head. Yes, I'm touching the bottom. Why?"

"Because I'm coming in, too. You know, the buddy system."

She heard a splash. The water sloshed against her.

"Scout Swimming Rule Number One, never go in the water without a buddy."

"What about the troop?" she asked in a whisper, as he reached her side and pulled her toward him.

"Let 'em find their own buddies," he said with a growl, and brought her against his body, bare skin to bare skin. And suddenly the water wasn't so cool anymore.

In the darkness Katherine spread the soap over Danny's body, recklessly allowing herself to enjoy his response to her touch. She knew that being together in the lake with no restraints was a risk in every way. But she couldn't say no to his demands. She never could.

Maybe she couldn't stop him from leaving. If loving him wasn't enough, there was nothing she could do. She'd just have to make him see how important it was for him to be with Mike, for them to be together as a family. If it took building a campfire and cooking biscuits in an iron pan, fine, she'd do it. By the time they'd dried off and Katherine had pulled on her jeans and shirt, she felt much better. "Beans and biscuits, bring them on," she said.

Only she knew that at the bottom of her pack was a secret supply of cupcakes and soda.

Eight

Faces pink and scrubbed, water dripping from their wet hair, Katherine and Danny walked back toward the campfire, meeting Nancy and an assignment of dishwashers en route to the river.

"So I was wrong," Nancy whispered in passing. "I guess I never knew what a natural talent you have for being devious."

"Oh? I'm sure I don't know what you mean," Katherine said, rubbing her hair briskly with her towel.

"Don't kid me. Damp hair, starry eyes? These campers might not know, but I can recognize a satisfied man when I see one. And the woman with him is practically purring, too. Don't worry, Katherine, the kids didn't even miss you."

Maybe not, but Katherine felt herself blush. Being with Danny was one thing, but this great sexual appetite they had for each other seemed to be growing. Neither was content unless they were touching, and it was rapidly becoming addictive.

Back at the campsite Danny filled paper plates

with what looked suspiciously like crumbled hamburgers, and a chunk of burned skillet bread. He handed one plate to Katherine and kept one for himself. They sat side by side, eating, giving every appearance of paying close attention to the fire safety discussion taking place around the campfire.

As Katherine finished her food the Scoutmaster swung into an enthusiastic chorus of ninety-nine bottles of pop on the wall. As the song finally wound down, he began telling a story, a very scary ghost story that immediately caught the group's attention. By the time several other adults joined in, serious yawns were heard among the Scouts and more than one pair of eyelids were trying to close.

"Okay, guys, that's it." The leader stood and began to give orders for banking the fire for the night. He assigned the cook detail for the morning meal and made certain that every camper was settling down for the night.

As Katherine looked around she saw Mike heading toward her.

"Good night, Katherine," he said shyly. "Thanks for being such a good sport."

"I've enjoyed it," she admitted, "but I'm not sure what I'm supposed to do now. I mean, do we change to pajamas?"

"Not necessary," Danny answered as he came up behind her. "Night, Mike, sleep tight. Katherine and I are going for a walk. We'll be back in a few minutes."

He glanced around, slid his hand into Katherine's, and began stepping backward in the darkness.

"What are you doing, Danny?" she whispered.

"I'm just going to give you a few safety instructions," he whispered back, "about life in the woods." But there was nothing safe about the good-night kiss he gave her when they reached the darkness beneath the trees.

By the time she returned to her tent, Katherine was sure that she was too wound up to sleep. She wasn't. She didn't think she moved until the sound of campers eating breakfast woke her.

After a morning of learning to tie knots and identify trees and birds, it was decided that the boys could take a short swim before hiking back. For a time the boys splashed around in the shallow water near the bank, tossing a beach ball back and forth. Katherine and Danny sat on a fallen tree trunk, not touching, yet content to watch their son interacting with the other children.

Suddenly there was a shout. Katherine looked up and saw Mike struggling frantically, his head bobbing beneath the surface as his hands slapped the water. The current had suddenly turned violent.

"Boys, get out of the water, quick!" the Scoutmaster called. "They've opened the dam upriver."

Danny jumped in and started toward the boy. Katherine, without a thought, followed in and began helping to pull the other children from the river. She glanced back to see Mike still thrashing in the water, calling frantically for help. Danny, neck-high in the water, seemed frozen. Belatedly they heard a shrill whistle.

"Oh, God!" Katherine realized that Danny hadn't moved. Now she couldn't see Mike at all. Everybody knew that the dam was opened periodically to allow the overflow to run off. But the opening was always preceded by a very loud, continuous whistle that alerted fishermen and residents downstream. Except the whistle hadn't blown early enough today, and Mike was being swept away while Danny stood watching.

"Danny, help me!" Katherine dived out into the rushing water and headed for the spot where Mike had been. She could hear someone behind her. But the current was too fast. She couldn't fight it. Where was he? Where was her son?

Her heart pounded in her ears. The water blinded her and filled her mouth so that she couldn't even call out. Mike! she screamed silently. Where are you?

Then she saw him up ahead, his head just above the waterline, dipping under and popping back to the surface. She drew on some inner strength and quickened her stroke, working her way to him inch by exhausting inch until she could reach out and draw his chin toward her.

"Don't fight me, Mike!" she yelled.

But he continued to struggle frantically. He was past hearing or understanding what she was saying. She had to get his attention or he would die. They could both die now in the river, which had come to mean so much to Danny.

"Mike!" she screamed. "Mike! Don't fight me!

I'm your mother and I'll save you. Your mother! I'm your real mother. Do you understand? I've got you. Just relax!" Finally Mike let himself go limp, and Katherine started swimming toward the shore. Slowly she made progress until at last she could touch bottom. The Scout leader leapt from the bank and took Mike from her just as she reached the end of her reserve.

He was safe. Mike was safe. She'd saved her son.

Suddenly her arms were like soft noodles in the current. She could barely lift her feet and pull herself toward the bank. At that moment Katherine stepped into a hole, and she went under. The plunging current reached out and jerked her back into the river again. By the time she fought her way to the surface, she knew she didn't have the strength to save herself.

"Danny? Help me!" she called out weakly. Where was Danny? Why didn't he come? Dimly she recalled his stopping and watching as Mike was swept away. She couldn't seem to find her footing. In the swirling water and debris, she went under again. There was nothing she could do. Water rushed into her mouth as she screamed. She was going to die. Dark River was going to kill her. Why didn't Danny come?

Then she felt herself being lifted. Two familiar arms pulled her across a log, holding her with a grip of steel.

"Katherine! Katherine, I've got you," he screamed. "I'm sorry. Please, trust me, Katie darling."

"Danny?"

"Yes, I'm here."

He hadn't left her. Mary Manley had been wrong.

The log bobbled and tore away downriver carrying them both. It plunged across now-submerged rocks, playing a game of tag with logs and other pieces of wood. At one point Katherine was flung against something cold and hard. A burning pain ripped across her shoulder. Afterward she didn't know if she'd been knocked out, or if she'd fainted. But when she opened her eyes again, she was in her own bed with three sets of anxious eyes looking down on her.

"What's wrong?" she whispered, her throat tight and dry.

"Katherine?" Aunt Vic said in an anxious voice.

"Darling?" It was Danny's strained voice.

"Mother?" Mike's voice was filled with relief.

She heard them all, but the only voice that registered belonged to Mike. He was all right. He hadn't drowned. And he'd—he'd called her mother. He knew the truth at last.

Suddenly everything came rushing back. The river, the water crashing over her. Danny! Confusion swept over her, and she struggled to sit up.

"No, Katherine, don't try to move." Danny's voice came from somewhere in the rolling blanket of fog that threatened to overtake her.

"You must be still," Aunt Vic was saying. "You've got a cut on your arm that had to be stitched, but the doctor said you're going to be fine. They've given you something to make you rest."

Gingerly she lay back, feeling the pull of her stitches. Her body was one big ache. Her thinking was fuzzy. She didn't want to sleep. Not now. There was something she didn't understand, something that she had to know. Then Mike was leaning over her, holding her hand as if he were afraid that she were going to run away.

"You pulled me out," he said, his face pale and worried. "You jumped in the water and swam after me. I didn't know you could do that."

"Neither did I," she replied weakly. "You were very brave to trust me."

His eyes were big and filled with unmistakable joy. "Of course I'd trust my mother," he whispered, "my real mother came and got me, didn't she? Just like my grandmother said she would."

Katherine nodded and closed her eyes. She couldn't speak, her heart was so full. Then everything began to fade into a warm, happy feeling. She was safe. Mike was safe. Trust. There was trust in the room where there'd been only guilt and confusion. There was nothing to worry about, not anymore.

When she opened her eyes again, there was nobody there but Danny. He was sitting in a chair, his elbows resting on the edge of her bed, his hands covering his face.

"Danny?"

He didn't answer. All she could hear was his breathing.

"Danny, are you all right?"

"No, I'm not all right," he said in a low, hoarse voice. "I almost let our son drown."

"What do you mean?" Her arm snaked from beneath the sheet and grasped Danny's arm, stripping it from his face. He was crying. With a groan he laid his head across her stomach, and she felt the jerking of his body as he wept.

"He's fine, Danny. We're all fine."

"But, Katherine. I just stood there and let him be swept away. I couldn't move. You were the one to jump in and get him. I couldn't save my own son."

"But, Danny, that happens sometimes. People panic and they literally can't perform. He would never hold that against you, and neither would I."

"Don't you see, Katherine? He'll never be able to trust me. You may not think so now, but you won't be able to trust me either. I love you so much, I'd die for you, but I won't be able to make this right. You were right about me all along. I'll always let you down."

He stood up and looked at Katherine for a long moment. Then he whirled around and left the room. Katherine heard his footsteps on the stairs. Moments later she heard a car engine start up, and then the world was silent.

The river had started it all.

Because of it, she'd reclaimed her son.

Because of it, she'd lost Danny.

* * *

For three days Katherine was forced to stay in bed. She alternated between complete happiness with her son and total despair over Danny's disappearance. Why had he gone? Where could he be? She couldn't eat. She couldn't sleep. Worst of all, she couldn't even ask where he was.

Finally Aunt Vic insisted on a showdown. "What exactly do you plan to do with the rest of your life?" she asked in sharp, unconcealed disgust. "Hide up here and let him leave? Don't make the mistake I did with your father, Katherine."

"My father? What do you mean?" Katherine asked. "I don't understand."

"I fell in love with your father, Katherine, and there was a time when I think he cared for me, too. But he didn't know how to get past the gossip that would have occurred. He let his fear of besmirching the Sinclair reputation come between us. So I stayed in the guest house, and he stayed in the big house for all the years that he lived. I know now that in trying to shut out his desire for me, he closed you out, too. Don't let that happen to you."

Aunt Vic and her father? It was beginning to make sense, that niggling thought she'd always had about her father's reaction to her aunt—two people who could have been happy together if they'd only reached out for each other. But that didn't have anything to do with Danny and her, did it?

"Danny's already gone, Aunt Vic."

"Yes, all the way back to the Dark River Inn."

"He's at the Inn?" Her heart suddenly soared.

"Yes, but I don't think he's going to wait for you very long. If you love him, go after him."

Katherine wanted to rush to the Inn, but Danny's words kept coming back to her. Finally she repeated her fears. "But, Aunt Vic, he stood there and watched Mike almost drown. How could a father who cared about his child do that?"

"The man can't swim, Katherine."

"Danny can't swim?"

"No," Aunt Vic said, "he apparently never learned."

Katherine was stunned. Of course, it made sense. His father couldn't swim. He had no one to teach him. That's why Danny hadn't been able to save Mike. But he tried. He'd done his best. It hadn't been his fault.

"Why didn't he say anything?"

"Because he was ashamed. Don't you see, he was a failure before you, before Mike, before Dark River. The old feelings just took over again."

"Oh, Aunt Vic, I didn't blame him. I love him. I always have, no matter what he is."

"You ought to," she agreed, "he risked his own life to save you."

Then it all came rushing back, the water closing over her head, the arms pulling her from the water and holding her over a log as the churning water carried them away. Danny's arms. She'd trusted him just as she always had. Why hadn't she ever understood that before?

She'd lost Danny, and rather than risk reaching out to him, she'd hidden behind her concern for Mike. Mike would have accepted the truth in the beginning. It was her own fear of rejection that kept her from telling him she was his mother and Danny was his father. She was afraid that Mike would choose Danny over her.

But no more. She intended to have her son and Danny Dark, and this time she intended to shout the truth from the rooftop.

Katherine dressed, and drove downtown, her mind quickly assimilating the official duties she would have to perform. She'd quickly settle the annual celebration of the final days of the Revolution that was coming up, and the matter of the plant. Afterward, she'd deal with Danny. He might think he was skipping out on her, but this time she had news for him.

"Well, it's about time, boss," Nancy said, concern evident on her face. "Heavens, you look awful."

"Thanks, Nancy. That helps a lot. Tell me what's happening."

"Well, Danny has just about everything worked out. Once I finish typing the papers, we'll be back together again."

Katherine stopped her forward progress. "What did you say?"

"The papers that give the land back to Dark River," Nancy said, drawing her attention back to her computer. "The council has already accepted his plan for the new plant. The bank has the funds, and we're setting up an employment office down at the Senior Citizens Center."

"Senior Citizens Center? That sounds like a strange place to handle the employment."

"Not if the employees are going to be senior citizens," Nancy said with a smile. "Ah, Katherine, this man of yours is the best thing to happen to Dark River since old Shotgun Sinclair."

Senior citizens? Their new plant would employ the older people in Dark River? Why hadn't she ever considered such an idea? It was a perfect solution to most of their problems, and it satisfied the opponents as well as those who wanted to bring in more tax revenue. And Danny had done it.

"I know this must make some sense, Nancy, but I don't think I understand. Where is Danny now?"

"In your office. By the way, I think he'd make a good replacement for you, if you decide to retire one of these days. Or maybe we could have a co-mayorship. That would be a first, wouldn't it?"

"Why on earth should I decide to retire?" Katherine was delaying the upcoming confrontation by asking questions that she didn't need answered. Her attention was drawn to her closed office door. If she understood Nancy correctly, Danny was behind it, in her office, at her desk, doing her job.

"Well, I thought that since you're getting married, maybe you might decide to retire when you two get back from your honeymoon."

"Our honeymoon," Katherine repeated woodenly.

"When Mary Manley told me that the tickets Danny bought were part of a honeymoon package to Cancun, Mexico, I just about flipped out. And if that wasn't enough, the next leg of the trip is for four. He's taking all of you to Disney World. I can understand a family trip like that. What I don't understand is why you never told me Mike was your son. I'm hurt."

"Honeymoon? Disney World? Go take a coffee break, Nancy. I'll apologize later."

"But I . . . Yes, ma'am."

Katherine put her hand on the doorknob and turned it slowly. She pushed open the door and walked inside. Danny hung up the phone and looked up at her.

"What honeymoon package to Cancun, Danny?"

"Don't worry, Katherine, after what happened, I'm going to cancel it."

"Oh? Why?"

"I think we both know why. I've had the papers prepared to officially deed the land to Dark River. I'll be finished with the details in a couple of days and be out of here."

"Uh-huh. And what about Mike?"

"What about him? He's where he wants to be. He's content to stay here with his mother and Aunt Vic. We've already discussed the situation. I think you ought to know that I told him I'm his real father. He understands what happened when he was born."

"But he's never said a word."

"I know. We—he was worried about you. You've been acting so distant."

"And what happens when you return from Saudi Arabia?"

"Oh, that. I've canceled all that. There are others I can send. I thought I'd find myself a place in Savannah. I'll be close enough so that Mike can visit when he likes."

"You've solved the town's problems. You're solving Mike's. All this without discussing it with me?"

"After what happened," he said softly, "I rather thought that you wouldn't want to hear anything I had to say."

"I see." Katherine walked around the desk and walked over to the window overlooking the square. "Now you're going to disappear again?"

"Something like that, I guess."

"Wrong. Not this time, Danny Dark. You seem to have an answer for righting every wrong except one. And that's a grievance you are totally and completely responsible for."

"I don't understand."

"You make me fall in love with you, and then you decide that you're not good enough for me and disappear. Well, not this time, Mr. Dark. I let that happen once, but not again. We are getting married. We're going to be a family—you, me, Aunt Vic, Mike, and the children we're going to have."

Katherine turned around and leaned against the windowsill, her arms crossed defiantly across her chest. "And if you try to leave, I'll have you arrested. I'm the mayor and I can do it—if necessary."

Danny stared at Katherine in disbelief. "You aren't serious?"

"Think not?"

Danny covered the distance between them in an instant.

"You're not kidding?"

"Not at all. The only place you're going is home, with me, until we can plan a wedding ceremony. We're getting married on the square in the park during the Founder's Day festivities in front of the entire town."

His first coherent thought was that the same rock that had cut her shoulder had addled her brains. "You can't be serious, Katherine."

She lifted her arms and drew him close, wincing slightly at the pull of her stitches. "I'm very serious, Danny."

"Don't hurt yourself, darling," he said quickly, lowering her arms to a position around his waist. He felt her tremble slightly, and he badly needed to dispel the awkward feeling that had suddenly come between them.

"What's wrong?" Katherine asked with a frown on her face.

"I'm afraid, Katherine, afraid that I won't be able to make you happy."

"Danny, the only times in my life I've ever truly been happy have been when I was with you. I know now that there is no happiness for me without you. Don't leave me again."

When she looked up at him with the morning sun beaming over her shoulders like a curtain of gold, what he saw was trust. What he saw was love. Danny felt a warmth inside his heart that swelled and began to radiate throughout his entire body. The warmth was a reflection of the love in Katherine's eyes.

"Leave you? I've never left you, Katherine. Wherever I've gone, you've been there with me."

Their kiss was urgent, emotions taking over from their being apart for almost a week. She had never felt so good, felt so right in his arms before.

Finally he drew back. "Yes, if you're sure, I'll marry you, Katherine Sinclair, in an official ceremony before the world. It will only make our being together legal. For in truth, I married you a long time ago."

She leaned against him, content to feel the strength of his presence. A chorus of "Whoopee!" suddenly filled the silence.

"What in heaven's name?" She turned around.

In the square below, townspeople had gathered.

"Congratulations, Katherine," a representative called out. "The citizens of Dark River are glad to have a leader who knows how to get her man."

The square was thronging with people. Booths had been set up by the civic organizations and church groups in the area, offering every conceivable kind of food. In the gazebo a band was playing, a bit off key, but with great enthusiasm. Three-legged races and tugs-of-war for the children had been completed. The reenactment of the mock founding of the town of Dark River was about to begin.

But first, Joe Hall, clad in the rough suit of a Revolutionary War patriot, walked up to the microphone on the bandstand and waited while the band gave a rather interesting drum-and-trumpet roll.

As the crowd began to quiet, Joe spoke.

"Ladies and gentlemen, you are hereby invited to participate in a reenactment of our past and a celebration of our faith in the future. Today we, the citizens of Dark River, are witnesses to righting a wrong that has been perpetuated in our city for over two hundred years."

The crowd began to draw closer to listen.

"The healing of the wound and the promise of the future begins with a wedding this day between Katherine Elizabeth Sinclair and Daniel Dark. Please join them in this joyous occasion."

The band began to play the wedding march.

From the city hall building Katherine stepped out into the sunshine and took the arm of the man waiting there.

He looked down at her, his great dark eyes filled with emotion. "I hope you know what we're doing, Katherine. Are you sure this crowd wouldn't just as soon see a lynching?"

Katherine laughed merrily. "Oh, you wonderful man. No, this crowd isn't interested in anything but a wedding. But perhaps your fears will make you appreciate my wedding gift even more."

"What gift?" Danny asked, holding her arm

even tighter. "There's nothing you can give me that will make me prouder than I already am."

He'd always known she was an angel, but now, in the sunlight, wearing a strapless white wedding gown of satin and lace, Danny felt his heart swell.

The crowd parted, forming a corridor through which they passed. They walked across the green, up the steps, and into the gazebo, where the minister, Mike, and Aunt Vic were waiting.

Before the entire population of the city of Dark River, Katherine Sinclair became Danny Dark's wife. Afterward, he kissed her gently, sweetly, then they turned to face the crowd and waited to watch the Founder's Day ceremonies.

Joe Hall stepped back to the microphone and began the telling. "This reenactment will be different," he explained. "During the last few weeks we've managed to uncover new information about the founding of our city, and I think that you'll find it very interesting.

"On December twenty-seventh, 1778," he went on, "the notorious Shotgun Sinclair was holed up on the bank of the river, waiting for his chance to raid the rich planters gathered in Savannah. He had secretly formed an alliance with the English, who planned to invade the port city. Fort Sunberry fell on January tenth, with Savannah following shortly thereafter. The last stronghold, the proud little settlement of Augusta, was defeated by the thirty-first. The patriot leaders were forced to hide."

There was a gasp that rippled throughout the

crowd. Joe paused for the excited comments that followed. Danny looked down at Katherine, his gaze questioning. What was Katherine up to? Were they rewriting history on this hot summer afternoon?

"But the fleeing patriots made a decision," Joe said, bringing quiet to the square again. "They sent one of their own officers to rout out the turncoat Sinclair, and bring him to justice. Here now is the true story of the founding of Dark River."

Across the square came a group of drunken rioters, pulling a wagon piled high with goods. The man on the large horse in front came to a stop in the middle of the square and slid to the ground.

"We make camp here, men, by this black river. Those rag-tailed soldiers will never find us here. Tomorrow, we again fight alongside the English, and afterward," he chuckled, "we'll lay claim to anything they leave behind."

The crowd gasped.

Shots rang out as a group of men on horseback rode into the clearing and surrounded the drunken men.

Leading the charge was a tall, dark-haired patriot officer. "Drop your weapons, Shotgun Sinclair," he said in a voice that left no room for argument. "You're under arrest."

"Says who?"

"I do. I'm Captain Daniel Dark, and this is my land you're soiling with your presence."

"How say you?" the older man standing on the ground asked with a glance at his men. "This be my land, straight from the king himself, all that land from the river to the west. I have a paper that says it."

"A paper issued by the men you sold out to, no doubt," the captain said quietly. "My grant is from the governor of Georgia himself, Sinclair. You can claim whatever of the rest you want, but the land from the hill you're standing on to the river is mine."

"Yeah!" a chorus of agreement and nodding of heads came from the men on horseback. "This river belongs to Daniel Dark."

"Not so," Sinclair argued, standing straight now before his enemy. "The only way you'll get this land is to kill me for it."

"I'll not kill you, Sinclair. You're to be tried as a traitor, before a jury of your own kind."

"I think not, Dark. This will be settled now, between the two of us." The actor portraying Shotgun Sinclair suddenly pulled a small pistol from his coat and fired it at Daniel's head. The shot appeared to miss, but the actor on the horse fell to the ground. What transpired thereafter was an engrossing representation of Shotgun Sinclair wounding Daniel David Dark and being subsequently strung up from the nearest tree by Daniel's followers.

One of the patriots spoke. "Hence forth, from this time forward, this land belongs to our leader, Captain Dark, and we declare this river to be called Dark River in his honor."

"And that, ladies and gentlemen," Joe concluded solemnly, "is the truth of what happened over two hundred years ago, right here on the square in Dark River. It came from the diary of one of the citizens who lived here and witnessed history in the making." Joe's speech ended with a roll of the drums, and the crowd began to applaud wildly.

Danny felt Katherine's fingers press against his arm. He made a move toward the microphone.

"No, Danny," she whispered, "it's the truth. Mike and I found it in an old diary. Dark River belongs to Danny Dark, and it always has. This truth is my wedding gift to you. Now, it's your turn."

"My turn?" he repeated, his mind still whirling with what he'd just heard.

"Your wedding gift to the town, remember?"

"Oh, yes." Danny stepped up to the microphone and waited for the noise to die down. "Ladies and gentlemen, I have to tell you that what you've just seen came as a complete surprise to me. My father always told me that Dark River belonged to the Darks. But I never really believed him. I'm sorry now that I didn't. However," he drew himself up, and stood very tall in the midday sun. "However, on this most auspicious occasion, I have my own announcement to make."

The crowd took a step forward. Confusion and uncertainty clouded their faces.

"As my wedding gift to my wife and my town, I'm signing ownership of the land in question over to the city. All I ask is that I'm allowed to be a part of this—and you."

A loud roar of approval broke out as the band

began a chorus of "For He's A Jolly Good Fellow." This time when Danny took Katherine in his arms, his kiss was neither brief nor sweet. In fact, by the time they broke apart, Katherine couldn't hear the catcalls of the crowd for the thunder of her heart.

"About that honeymoon, Danny," she asked breathlessly, "when does it start?"

"Tomorrow," he answered, just as breathless.

"But, Danny, I don't know if I can wait."

"I don't intend for us to, darling." He smiled wickedly. "Come with me. Right now we have one more historical event to replay."

"Oh, where is that?"

"Under a tree by the river," he answered, lifting her into his arms and walking toward his car.

"Oh, yes," she agreed, and laid her head against his chest. "Are we prepared?" she asked shyly.

"Absolutely not," he replied. "This is an official, historically accurate reenactment. I have the piece of paper that makes it so. For now and forever, all the world knows that Katherine Sinclair is Danny Dark's girl."

Epilogue

"Aunt Vic, look what I have?"

Mike ran across the square, proudly displaying his prize. It was a replica of the statue of General Sinclair.

"What are you going to do with that?" Aunt Vic asked curiously. "It really isn't any good anymore, is it?"

"Of course it is," he replied seriously. "It's part of my mother's history. I'm going to put it in the train garden. You did say that every Sinclair added something new to the garden, didn't you? And I'm a Sinclair now, too, aren't I?"

"Yes, they did until your grandfather's time. And yes, you certainly are, Michael Sinclair Dark."

"Well, that's what I want to do. I want to build the park by the river and put General Sinclair right in the middle of it."

"But, Mike, General Sinclair wasn't really a man to be respected. Won't that make your father feel bad?"

"Gosh, no. Since my dad saved my mom's life,

the town thinks that he's a real hero. And now that my mother and my father are married, he's a Sinclair, too, isn't he? I mean the minister said that two would become one," he said proudly. "What do you think, Aunt Vic?"

"I think," she said with a smile, "that tradition is a fine idea. Forgive me, Sam," she said with a wink at the statue of Shotgun Sinclair, "but there are times when historical accuracy has to be sacrificed for the good of all."

"What does that mean, Aunt Vic?"

"It just means that young girls sometimes allow themselves a bit of exaggeration when they're writing in their diaries. If I were a young girl in 1790 who was in love with an outlaw, I'd make him a hero, too. Two hundred years later, who's going to know whether or not a diary is accurate. By the way, Mike, remind me to stop by the river on the way home."

"Why, Aunt Vic?"

"Oh, I have an old ledger that I want to throw away. The history of Dark River is now official, and I rather like this version, don't you?"

The Dark River flowed silently and swiftly past the city square toward the sea.

Hidden beneath a giant live oak, Katherine and Danny Dark lay, entwined in each other's arms, loving each other, by their river, where first they'd learned to love, so long ago.

THE EDITOR'S CORNER

Each month we have LOVESWEPTs that dazzle . . . that warm the heart or bring laughter and the occasional tear—all of them sensual and full of love, of course. Seldom, however, are all six books literally sizzling with so much fiery passion and tumultuous romance as next month's.

First, a love story sure to blaze in your memory is remarkable Billie Green's **STARBRIGHT,** LOVESWEPT #456. Imagine a powerful man with midnight-blue eyes and a former model who has as much heart and soul as she does beauty. He is brilliant lawyer Garrick Fane, a man with a secret. She is Elise Adler Bright, vulnerable and feisty, who believes Garrick has betrayed her. When a terrifying accident hurls them together, they have one last chance to explore their fierce physical love . . . and the desperate problems each has tried to hide. As time runs out for them, they must recapture the true love they'd once believed was theirs—or lose it forever. Fireworks sparked with humor. A sizzler, indeed.

Prepare to soar when you read LOVESWEPT #457, **PASSION'S FLIGHT,** by talented Terry Lawrence. Sensual, sensual, sensual is this story of a legendary dancer and notorious seducer known throughout the world as "Stash." He finds the woman he can love faithfully for a lifetime in Mariah Heath. Mariah is also a dancer and one Stash admires tremendously for her grace and fierce emotionality. But he is haunted by a past that closes him to enduring love—and Mariah must struggle to break through her own vulnerabilities to teach her incredible lover that forever can be theirs. This is a romance that's as unforgettable as it is delectable.

As steamy as the bayou, as exciting as Bourbon Street in New Orleans, **THE RESTLESS HEART,** LOVESWEPT #458, by gifted Tami Hoag, is sure to win your heart. Tami has really given us a gift in the hero she's created for this romance. What a wickedly handsome, mischievous, and sexy Cajun Remy Doucet is! And how he woos heroine Danielle Hamilton. From diapering babies to kissing a lady senseless, Remy is masterful. But a lie and a shadow stand between him and Danielle . . . and only when a dangerous misunderstanding parts them can they find truth and the love they deserve. Reading not to be missed!

Guaranteed to start a real conflagration in your imagination is extraordinary Sandra Chastain's **FIREBRAND,** LOVESWEPT #459. Cade McCall wasn't the kind of man to answer an ad as mysterious as Rusty Wilder's—but he'd never needed a job so badly. When he met the green-eyed rancher whose wild red hair echoed her spirit, he fell hard. Rusty found Cade too handsome, too irresistible to become the partner she needed. Consumed by the flames of desire they generated, only searing romance could follow . . . but each feared their love might turn to ashes if he or she couldn't tame the other. Silk and denim . . . fire and ice. A LOVESWEPT that couldn't have been better titled—**FIREBRAND**.

Delightful Janet Evanovich outdoes herself with **THE ROCKY ROAD TO ROMANCE,** LOVESWEPT #460, which sparkles with fiery fun. In the midst of a wild and woolly romantic chase between Steve Crow and Daisy Adams, you should be prepared to meet an old and fascinating friend—that quirky Elsie Hawkins. This is Elsie's fourth appearance in Janet's LOVESWEPTS. All of us have come to look forward to where she'll turn up next . . . and just how she'll affect the outcome of a stalled romance. Elsie won't disappoint you as she works her wondrous ways on the smoldering romance of Steve and Daisy. A real winner!

Absolutely breathtaking! A daring love story not to be missed! Those were just a couple of the remarks heard in the office from those who read **TABOO,** LOVESWEPT #461, by Olivia Rupprecht. Cammie Walker had been adopted by Grant Kennedy's family when her family died in a car crash. She grew up with great brotherly love for Grant. Then, one night when Cammie came home to visit, she saw Grant as she'd never seen him before. Her desire for him was overwhelming . . . unbearably so. And Grant soon confessed he'd been passionately in love with her for years. But Cammie was terrified of their love . . . and terrified of how it might affect her adopted parents. **TABOO** is one of the most emotionally touching and stunningly sensual romances of the year.

And do make sure you look for the three books next month in Bantam's fabulous imprint, FANFARE . . . the very best in women's popular fiction. It's a spectacular FANFARE month with **SCANDAL** by Amanda Quick, **STAR-CROSSED LOVERS** by Kay Hooper, and **HEAVEN SENT** by newcomer Pamela Morsi.

Enjoy!

Sincerely,

Carolyn Nichols

Carolyn Nichols,
Publisher,
LOVESWEPT
Bantam Books
666 Fifth Avenue
New York, NY 10103